Bad Company

Tori Minard

Bad Company

Copyright 2014 Tori Minard

Cover by Tori Minard from photos by Daniel Sroga and Steve Allen

Enchanted Lyre Books

Chapter 1
Devil's Coming

Gage:

My condo looked like it belonged in a spread in Architectural Digest Magazine, or some other shelter mag. I'd had it professionally decorated because, you know, A-list movie star. We were expected to have luxe surroundings.

Not that I really gave a shit, but hell I had the money, so why not?

The bedroom had slate-gray walls and a platform bed made of some kind of exotic black wood, everything understated, ultra-modern, masculine. It cost me a fucking fortune, but whatever. It looked good. I looked good. That was all that mattered in this town.

At the moment, it was dark, chilly with air-conditioning. My hair, still wet from a shower at the gym, made my scalp cold in the breeze coming from the A.C.. The air smelled flat, but at least it didn't reek with exhaust fumes like so much of the outdoors around here.

Through the windows, the lights of L.A. twinkled at me, pretending to beauty that daylight would prove totally fake and winking at their own joke. So much of this town was like that. Fakery and illusion. Including me.

I sauntered across all the open floor space toward my walk-in closet. The bedroom, huge as it was, had almost no furniture. Just the bed, a long black dresser, a sling chair, two crazy nightstand table things with all these freaky angles. My designer loved the damn things.

The lamps by the bedside were wall-mounted, tubular light-dildoes. Again, the designer loved them. I didn't care as long as they allowed me to see what the hell I was doing. Not that I did much in here. Sleep and fuck basically summed it up.

And I never let a woman spend the night or do more than doze for a few. I didn't do girlfriends and I didn't do overnights. Maybe that sounds like typical young male posturing, especially from a movie star of my status. But the thing is I wasn't good for anything more than a couple of encounters.

The most important thing to know about me is this: when I was ten years old, my mom made a deal with the devil.

Seriously. I shit you not.

Right in the living room of our cheap-ass apartment. You've heard those stories about people calling up Old Nick at some lonely country crossroads, right? But my mom didn't bother with that. She summoned him at an altar set up on our entertainment center, right next to our dying TV.

My dad, in case you're wondering, had nothing to do with it. He took off when I was three and I haven't seen him since. I don't even remember him.

Nowadays, I didn't live in that shithole anymore. We'd come up in the world since. That deal had propelled me into the movie business.

My career had moved slowly at first but I'd worked steadily, made a name for myself as a kid actor, then transitioned to adult roles, something a lot of child actors never manage. And for a variety of reasons, I strongly suspected The Deal had protected me from some nasty, child-molesting fuckheads who used their positions of power in the business to get what they wanted from vulnerable kids.

Some of my friends hadn't been so lucky. If you can call a deal with the devil luck.

Now I lived in a two-story luxury condo with an ocean view. My mom had her own place bought with my money, from a career I hadn't earned and didn't deserve.

I hadn't seen the old apartment with its cardboard walls in fifteen years.

Still, when my mom called me five minutes before I had to leave for an important Hollywood party, I knew the devil was on her mind again.

I hauled the phone out of my jeans pocket as I went to my walk-in closet—roughly the size of your average airport concourse, with shiny black woodwork—to find something to wear. My thumb hovered over the talk button as I weighed whether or not to answer. She'd already left seven messages on my voicemail, all of them about *him*. And although I couldn't do anything about the problem, I also knew she wouldn't stop pestering me and leaving those nagging messages until I picked up and talked to her.

Shit. Maybe I could make this conversation quick. I hit the talk button.

"Yeah?" I tried to keep the irritation out of my voice. She drove me nuts, but she was still my mom.

"Gage? Are you okay?"

"Yeah, Mom, of course I'm okay. Why wouldn't I be?"

"You didn't answer my messages."

I walked across my half-empty closet and started flipping through my shirts. "I've been busy."

"I want you to be extra careful, okay?" Her voice sounded kind of slurred, like she'd been drinking.

"Why? What's up?" I chose a charcoal-gray silk. That was as formal as I got. No suit jackets, but a silk shirt I could do.

"You know," my mom whispered. "It's *him.*"

"Who?" I knew, but I wanted to make her say it.

"You know. About The Deal. I'm worried about it."

I'd showered earlier, after a hard gym session, so all I needed was a change of clothes. Tucking the phone between my chin and my shoulder, I stripped my T-shirt off with my free hand. "Isn't it a little late to worry now?"

"It's never too late."

Huh. You could've fooled me. It seemed to me it was way too late to do anything about The Deal, like say not making the goddamn thing in the first place.

"Gage? Are you still there?"

I breathed in deeply through my nose. Patience. I needed patience. If I argued with her, we could be here all night, or until I hung up on her. "I'm here."

"He's going to come for you. Soon. I want you to be super careful."

"Mom, you've been drinking," I said, as calmly as I could. "Call me back when you're sober."

"How can you tell? Anyway, I've only had a few. I know what I'm talking about."

"Sure you do."

"That's no way to talk to your own mother." She was trying for parental dignity, but it was too late for that as well. Also hard to pull off when she was drunk.

I pictured her sitting at her kitchen table with a bottle of vodka and a cigarette, her hair messy and her makeup smeared. It was probably yesterday's makeup.

"I've gotta go," I said. "I'm already late."

"Everyone's late to those parties. Gage, I feel like you're not listening to me."

That's because I wasn't. I practically knew this lecture by heart. She could've just texted me with something like "devil lecture", and we wouldn't have had to talk at all.

"Your friend Jeremy," she said. "He's been in a lot of trouble lately."

I frowned as I skinned out of my jeans. "Yeah, but what does that have to do with the deal?"

Jeremy was my closest friend, a former child actor like me. Also like me, he played guitar and fooled around with the drums and we occasionally played together. He'd struggled with heroin addiction for years. His family and I had done interventions and nothing had stuck so far. He'd do okay for a while, then slip up and start using again. I was hoping this time would be the charm, the one that saved him.

3

She made an impatient noise. "Haven't you ever wondered if it's because of *him?* Maybe he's influencing Jeremy."

"Yeah, I'm sure he is."

"This isn't funny! He told me..." She started whispering again. "He told me you had to die before he could take your soul, and if he couldn't get to you then he'd go after the people around you. Maybe he's targeting Jeremy."

Most people would probably decide my mom was playing with only a partial deck at this point. I mean, nobody believes in this stuff anymore, right? Except a few snake-handler types, that is.

But I'd been there. When she called up Old Scratch, I'd been huddled in a corner of the living room between the couch and the side wall. Hunkered down, terrified, peering out from beneath the ratty blue throw blanket I'd dragged over my head as the only protection I could think of, my arms around the stuffed-toy rabbit I thought I'd grown out of.

He'd materialized right in our living room, looking just as real as any regular human being except for the way his eyes glowed red. My mom hadn't even flinched. She'd presented The Deal like she was a master Devil-negotiator, like she worked these contracts all the time. Probably because it hadn't been her soul on the line.

I'd seen *him.* I knew he was real.

"Jeremy just got out of rehab, Mom. He's doing much better than he has in years." I hoped. "I'm pretty sure the devil isn't after him."

"You don't know that." In the background, glass clinked and liquid gurgled. She was pouring herself another fucking drink. "He's tricky. And if he can't get you, he'll take out each of the people close to you. He could come after me."

Now we got to the point. This was what really terrified her. The loss of her own skin. Although I had to wonder why the devil would take Jeremy or my mother? Why not just go straight to me, if I was who he wanted? That was the part of this whole scenario that I didn't get.

"Would you like me to kill myself so you don't have to worry anymore?" My voice was dry as the desert.

"No! Of course not!" She actually sounded like I'd offended her. Maybe she was the one who should've gone into the acting trade. "I would never want you to hurt yourself. How can you even ask that?"

"You traded my soul for success."

There was a long pause. I took advantage of her silence to put on a fresh pair of black jeans. She stayed quiet so long I got my shirt tucked in and the jeans zipped and buttoned before she opened her mouth again.

"What else was I going to use?" she said in a small voice.

"You could have left the whole thing alone." Hell, she could have thought to ask me if I even wanted what she was after. It was my potential career, but she'd never even tried to find out if I wanted to be a star. Let alone if I thought selling my immortal soul for success would be a good trade.

"You're the most successful young actor in Hollywood," she said. "The whole world loves you."

"And none of it came to me naturally. It doesn't really belong to me. It's all because of your precious Deal."

"That isn't true. You're incredibly talented, Gage. You were always so good-looking and talented. Gifted."

I shoved my feet into black leather boots. "So why make The Deal at all then? The way you're talking, we didn't need it."

"Because success in Hollywood isn't just about looks and talent; it's about who you know. We didn't know anyone. We needed an advantage."

"Right. An advantage. Listen, Mom, I really have to go. I'm picking up Jer for the party."

She heaved a theatrical sigh. "Okay. But promise me you'll be careful."

"Sure, Mom."

I hung up with relief. Conversation done. It had gone on a bit longer than I'd wanted, but a victory nonetheless. Now I could go out, have a good time without her nagging voice in my ear.

The be-careful shit was ridiculous. There was nothing to be careful about because nothing had changed about The Deal. My life was exactly the same as it had been yesterday, and the day before yesterday, and the day before that.

The hair on the back of my neck prickled and I rubbed at it in irritation. It felt hot in here, like the AC needed to be turned up. A skinny worm of unease wriggled its way up my spine.

I rubbed my neck again. This was bullshit. My mom and her drunken worries were just messing with my head. Tonight I had work to do, and fun to enjoy afterward, and I was going to make the most of both.

Chapter 2
The Cabin

Nova:

The sky visible through the gorgeous green canopy of big-leaf maple and Douglas fir was a hot, bright cerulean blue to match the heat of the summer day outside the car. Inside, air conditioning blasted an arctic chill through the air. The radio played a tired old country song, the kind where the singer just keeps on havin' kids and the trailer roof is about to fall off and there's no food in the cupboard. It was the only channel that came through clearly in this tiny mountain town.

My mom's silver sedan grumbled up the steep country drive that led to our cabin, the low chassis scraping over the bumps, grooves, and epic potholes in the gravel road. Vine maple, chinquapin, and Oregon grape scratched against the sides of the car, dragging twiggy fingers over the surface like they were trying to hold back the invading vehicle, keep it from reaching the cabin. I winced at the thought of what that was probably doing to my mother's formerly pristine paint job.

Maybe I should have waited to get my old truck back from the mechanic's shop before I made my escape, but I'd been too impatient. My folks were going to deliver it to me in a couple of weeks.

Nothing of the cabin could be seen yet beyond the twists of the drive and the thickly overgrown forest underbrush. I rolled down my window, letting the heady scent of an Oregon mountain summer into the car, along with a healthy dose of hot summer air. It was even hotter in the valley I'd left behind.

I could smell my own sweat in spite of the air conditioning. Had I forgotten to put on antiperspirant this morning? Oops. Well, it didn't much matter since I'd be alone up here.

Nobody cares what a hermit smells like, right?

My mom tilted her head to the side and gave me one of those Mom Looks. You know the kind. The ones that say, without words, that you're making a mistake and if you were a reasonable human being you'd listen to her wise motherly advice, but she knows you're going to do what you want regardless and she's trying to be patient with you.

That look used to work on me. I'd cave and do whatever it was she wanted of me just to get her to quit staring at me.

She'd been giving me the look off and on the whole way from Portland. Hours of it. Wonderful, fun-filled hours of mom-induced guilt. Now we were finally here and she was apparently launching a last-ditch campaign to get me to change my mind about my plans for my near-future.

Nope. Her scheming wasn't going to work. All I had to do was hold out in the face of the guilt-shame cocktail she was trying to serve me until she got tired and went home by herself.

I drummed my fingers on the steering wheel, my gaze fixed on the front door of our family cabin. The log walls looked golden in the afternoon sun, the steeply pitched green metal roof blending in with the thick growth of Douglas firs that surrounded it. My mood lifted just looking at it, remembering all the happy summer vacations spent here during my childhood.

"We're here," I said, completely unnecessarily.

"I noticed."

"I'm going in."

She put her hand on my forearm. "Honey, are you sure you want to do this? You're going to be up here all alone."

"I'm sure, Mom," I said, with what I hoped was a confident smile.

She sighed and shook her head, a slow single shake. That was another of her heavy-hitters. The sigh. Accompanied by that sad, I'm worried and disappointed look, it used to floor me every time.

Honestly, I didn't know if this cabin thing would work out for me. Maybe I wouldn't be able to handle it. Maybe I'd change my mind in a few days or weeks and come home again with my tail between my legs. But I wouldn't find out if I didn't try, and I wanted to know if I could manage by myself.

Plus it was quiet up here. No-one I knew lived in the tiny nearby town of Subalpine and my ex-fiancé disliked what he called "redneck country" intensely. There would be no awkward run-ins here.

I opened my door. "Are you coming?"

"Nova—"

"Mom, I'll be fine. I'm a big girl." The air outside the car smelled sweet, the resinous scent of evergreens mixed with ripe berries and a hint of woodsmoke, like summer picnics and Christmas rolled into one. I got out, just to forestall more argument.

But my mom was tougher than that. She popped out of the passenger side of the car, ready for battle. "You've never lived on your own. I don't think camping out up here is a good way to start."

Good grief, the cabin had running water and electricity. It's not like I'd be living in a tent.

"Camping out? Come on, we've got one of the best cabins in the area." I grinned at her and dangled the cabin keys from my fingers. "It'll be great. Lots of fresh air."

"But what will you do up here all by yourself? You'll be lonely. And you're going to fall behind on your studies. You don't want to do that to yourself, do you?"

I wasn't going to be lonely. I liked solitude and I'd brought some art supplies so I could work, do some landscape sketches and nature studies. We'd already discussed this, about five hundred times. Why she felt the need to drag me over the coals again was beyond me. I guess she just couldn't believe I wouldn't fold, like I had all those other times.

"It's not too late to change your mind," she said hopefully. "We can drive back home right now. Or we can stay the night and go home in the morning. Your dad won't mind, and the girls will be thrilled."

My little sisters hadn't wanted me to do this either. Nobody did, except me. But nobody else had gone through what I had, either, and it wasn't their decision to make. Nobody else in the family was re-evaluating their whole life and reason for being. Not that I'm over-dramatic or anything.

"It's not like I'm moving to Mars," I said, going around to the trunk for my bags. "I have a phone. You guys can come up some weekends. I'll be home for holidays. It'll be fine."

My mom just shook her head. "I know you had a bad spring term, but that's no reason to hide out here like a hermit. There's no reason to jeopardize your future just because your boyfriend was a jerk."

Hauling my big, black suitcase out of the trunk, I turned toward the cabin. "I've made up my mind and I'm not going to argue with you about it. So unless you're not going to let me stay here after all, I'm going in."

They'd offered me the cabin when I'd proposed moving across the country. Apparently they'd rather have me in the family cabin, even if it was tucked away in the Cascade Mountains, than working my way across the country taking random waitressing jobs here and there and then moving on. That had been my first choice.

I wasn't very outgoing, so I don't know if the waitressing idea was really workable. But I'd had to get away. From everything.

When I'd walked in on my fiancé Barry and my so-called best friend Skylar doing the nasty in the living room of the apartment I shared with her, my world had turned inside-out in one second flat. Just the time it took me to comprehend what I was seeing. That moment changed everything. Made me question everything.

Was it me? Was I not enough woman for him? Was I too ugly, too fat, too thin, too shy, too brainy? What? Or was he just a weak-willed, cheating shit?

And Skylar—my best friend. How could she do it to me? It's not like she couldn't get her own guy; she had them following her around, dates every weekend. She had more guys than she knew what to do with and could have loaned out a few to her single friends. But no—she had to go after my fiancé.

I'd thought I knew them, that I knew myself. But I hadn't. And now I wasn't sure of anything, except that I had to get away. I'd turned into a total misanthropist, a hater of humankind. The only places that appealed to me were on top of mountains or maybe at the bottom of the ocean. Yeah. The ocean floor would be nice and quiet.

Peaceful. Completely free of cheating boyfriends and traitorous BFFs and people who thought they knew what I wanted better than I did. Only I didn't have access to any ocean-bottom retreats; what I did have was permission to use this old cabin.

I stuck the key in the lock and wiggled it. The knob was dusty. A thick layer of dust also lay on the nearby kitchen windowsill. Cobwebs festooned the lintel and the panes of glass in the window. Under the dirt, I could see the green paint flaking in a few places.

"Ugh," my mom said. "It's filthy."

"We haven't come up here for a long time." I opened the door to an interior covered in more dust, a thick yet fluffy layer of grunge that coated everything. The air smelled stale. Dead flies had sprinkled their tiny corpses throughout the dust, like raisins in a disgusting sort of raisin bran.

"Nova, you're not going to be happy here." She curled her lip as she stared at the floor. She'd dressed to help me move in, but her idea of casual clothes was freshly pressed dark-wash jeans and glossy new ballet flats, not the ratty sweats and old running shoes I'd chosen.

I glanced at her as I carted my suitcase into the living room. "Sure I will."

The truth was, I had no idea whether staying at the cabin would make me feel better or give me any clearer an understanding of myself. But I'd made up my mind and I wasn't changing it. Not until I'd given being on my own a shot. "Think of it like a retreat."

"It's not safe for you to be out here by yourself," she said in an ominous tone. "And you could do a retreat at a nice resort on the coast."

"Mom, I know how to take care of myself. I've got my mountain woman knife and everything. Plus I've got the pistol Dad gave me." And I knew how to use it. Dad and I had spent many hours at the shooting range practicing.

"That doesn't make me feel any better," she said, giving me the look again. "You know how I hate guns."

Nothing I said was going to make her feel good about this. "You're going to have to trust me. I'm not a kid anymore."

"We're going to visit you every weekend, you know. Otherwise we'll worry too much."

I set my case on the faded, brown couch and turned to make another trip to the car. "Just call first to make sure I'm here."

With any luck, she'd get royally sick of driving up here every single weekend and give me some distance. It would probably take her a few months to reach that point, though.

She took my hand as I passed her. "You don't have to quit school, you know. You could go closer to home."

"Yeah, I know. But this is what I want. I need some time to think about things." I drew away.

She trailed after me. My parents still thought I was going to graduate pre-med and go on to some prestigious medical school. They were doctors and that meant I should be one as well. Growing up, that had been my dream too, but now it was one more thing I wasn't so sure about. Maybe it had never been my dream, just one I'd taken on out of guilt.

Art, you know, is only for flakes. Sensible people make sensible plans, like becoming a doctor. They go to prestigious, private colleges like Pioneer and when they graduate, they've already been accepted into a well-regarded medical school. They sure don't hide out in an old cabin on a mountainside. They don't need to find themselves because they already know who they are.

I was not a sensible person.

"I hope that fiasco with Barry didn't make you doubt yourself," she said. "You're a bright girl and you have a great future ahead of you. Don't let the stupid things he and Skylar did ruin your chances for your career."

"Mom." I heaved a sigh an awful lot like hers. "I'm not ruining anything, okay? This is temporary."

Right. Temporary. And it wasn't guilt or shame or even worry I felt. Nope. I had every confidence this cabin experiment would turn out well and I'd prove my parents wrong.

Chapter 3
Overdose

Gage:

Jeremy's apartment complex had an underground parking lot and one of those inner courtyard things with a swimming pool and some decent but boring landscaping in the center. The outside of the place had a bland concrete wall around it, the green, blade-like leaves of some kind of spiky desert plant showing over the top. It looked a lot like a lot of other apartment complexes in the area. Nothing special.

I didn't take my mother's warning about *him* or Jeremy seriously. That Deal was fifteen years old already and I saw no reason to think it was coming due tonight. Why would it? There was nothing special about this evening, nothing unusual about the party we were going to or the people who'd be there. Just business as usual.

Except maybe that the party had a Bollywood theme and there were rumors they might have a Bengal tiger there. Maybe an elephant. And dancers, lots of Bollywood-style dancers. It sounded like a cross between a three-ring circus and an Indian epic movie.

But so what? Extravagant parties weren't that remarkable in my world.

The goal for this evening was to put in an appearance, make the rounds, then go cut loose with Jer. A fairly standard night for both of us.

Yet when I pulled up in the underground parking lot of Jeremy's place, something dark and uneasy moved through my belly. I took the stairs up to the courtyard garden, where I paused and stared up at his apartment building for a moment, trying to shake off the mood. He'd once owned a house, but his career had hit a low point with all his using, and he was renting an apartment now.

It was a nice enough place, but not even close to the luxury of the house he'd owned. The rooms were smaller and not as high-end. Jeremy didn't seem to care. He'd trash the place just like he had the house and every other home he'd ever occupied as long as I'd known him. His home was a party pad, and that was the extent of it.

I could see his apartment windows through thick fringes of palm fronds in the landscaped courtyard. The lights were on in his place and everything looked fine. Normal. My mom had just freaked me out with all that crap she threw at me.

Straightening my shoulders, I dashed up the concrete stairs to his door on the second floor and rang the bell. No-one answered, so I rang again. Heavy metal thundered right through the walls into the outside air. Someone had to be home.

But my second ring went unanswered. I banged my fist on the door. Nothing.

Maybe he was on the toilet. Pulling out my phone, I dialed him. His phone seemed to ring forever before finally sending me to his voicemail.

Damn it. We were going together so we could do the rounds later, when we'd gotten suitably bored and needed to find a better time. He knew I was coming over to pick him up. What the fuck was he doing up there?

Knowing him, he was banging a couple of chicks and had forgotten about the time. I shook my head and tried the door handle. It was open. That was weird in itself. I tried to tell myself there was nothing ominous about it; he'd just forgotten to lock up.

"Jer?" I stuck my head in the foyer.

The music was so loud he wasn't likely to hear me, so I shut the door and walked into his living room. Empty beer bottles littered the black leather couch, the chrome and glass coffee table, the tan plush carpet. No Jer and no girls.

That cold, heavy feeling snaked through my gut again. Even with all the noise from the music, there was something quiet about the place. Something unmoving and still. Empty.

I strode through the first floor rooms, all of them unoccupied. Take-out containers all over the place, still half full of food. The place smelled. Stank, actually. He had a cleaning lady, but apparently she hadn't come by yet.

Taking the stairs two at a time, I charged up to his room. The door stood open; the lights were on. Dirty clothes covered the fake wood floor and the fake black-leather club chair by the window. Clean underwear and T-shirts spilled out of his dresser drawers and an empty bottle of Gray Goose lay on its side on the rumpled bed.

The room stank of old sweat and alcohol. It smelled just as bad as downstairs, although I couldn't see any rotten food laying around.

"Jer? You here?" I called.

No answer.

The door to his bathroom stood open and the light was on inside. I could hear this steady drip-drip-drip sound, like someone hadn't turned the tap all the way off. Drip. Drip. Drip. And for some reason I can't explain, that sound told me everything. It told me things I didn't want to know.

My hands felt like ice blocks hanging from the ends of my arms. I forced myself to walk into the bathroom. Part of me was hoping, almost begging Fate that my worst suspicions weren't true as I moved with stiff legs through the open doorway.

His apartment had one of those modern sculptural tubs, a freestanding white one in an oval shape. It had always reminded me of a serving dish, the kind you fill with vegetables.

Jeremy lay in the tub. His eyes were half closed like he was going to sleep, but his face was blue. Greasy, unwashed blond hair lay flat on his scalp. The sculptural tap sticking out of the marble wall over the tub dripped water into the basin, one drop at a time. Drip. Drip. Drip.

One arm sprawled out over the edge of the tub, a piece of surgical hose still tied around his bicep. On the marble floor under his lax fingers lay a syringe. Empty. Next to it was an open bottle of expensive Scotch whiskey with half the liquor gone.

I rushed to him, as if hurrying could save him. But I already knew he was dead. I knew it before I touched his cold skin, before I felt the chill of the water, before I felt the side of his neck for a pulse.

"Jesus, Jer," I whispered. "What the fuck did you do to yourself?"

I pressed my fingertips to his neck again, just in case he did have a pulse and I'd missed it. But there was nothing. His body felt strange and I couldn't hear him breathing. How long had he been sitting there? It had to have been a while, considering how cold the water was. Jer wasn't the kind to sit in a tub of cold water on purpose.

I glanced at the counter. A small, orange prescription bottle lay on its side, the cap off, a couple of little white pills spilling out onto the gray marble counter.

Memories flooded me. All the times we'd partied together. The first time I'd ever shot heroin into a vein—Jer had shown me how to do it. Long nights talking and drinking, when secrets came out, ugly secrets I sometimes wish I'd never heard.

My skin prickled all over. There was this strange, heavy feeling in the air, almost like it was thicker than normal or pressing down on me. My head seemed to tingle inside.

Someone was in the room with me. I didn't feel alone anymore. The sense of dread I'd had before entering the bathroom intensified until it was almost unbearable. I swallowed hard and glanced reluctantly at my friend's corpse.

Naturally, he hadn't moved. Not at all. His cold blue eyes stared at the wall, glazed over and gone. There was nothing alive in him. Nothing at all. The sense of presence didn't come from Jeremy's body. It was something else.

An eerie sort of whispering came from the air, just beyond the edge of my hearing. As if someone were muttering one or two rooms over. The air seemed colder, too, as if the air conditioning had somehow dropped the temperature twenty degrees in an instant. I went back into the bedroom, but it was empty.

I needed to call someone about Jeremy. 911 or something. But not in the bathroom. Not in the bedroom, either. The atmosphere up here was growing denser and colder by the moment.

The presence seemed to watch me as I descended the stairs. I could feel its gaze on the back of my head. Was it *him?* Was my mother right?

Warm California air engulfed me as soon as I left the apartment, yet it brought little relief. I hate to admit it——I like to think I'm pretty much able to handle anything——but my hands shook a little and the hair on the back of my neck stood on end as I dragged my phone out again and called 911. Maybe my mom was right for once. Maybe *he* had been here.

Was this my fault, then? Was Jeremy dead because of me? Maybe if we'd never been friends, he wouldn't have OD'd. Maybe he'd never have used at all.

He used for reasons that had nothing to do with you.

Still. If it weren't for me—for the *Deal*—he might still be alive. Maybe the people who'd hurt Jer when we were kids would have hurt me instead. Maybe Jeremy would have been okay.

The *thing*, the presence, had followed me out into the night, yet it seemed weaker outside. I breathed easier and the hair on my neck settled.

I finished my call and stuck the phone in my pocket, glanced around, tried to get my bearings. Jeremy was dead. Dead. My best friend was dead and there seemed to be some kind of supernatural element to his death.

If my mom wasn't crazy, then whatever had killed Jer was after me and anyone close to me.

Jesus. What about my other friends? I had to find a way to protect them.

Chapter 4

House Party

Gage:

Central Oregon is dry. I'd heard that but didn't really believe it until I attended this house party in Sunriver and saw it for myself. Nothing but rolling red hills covered in sagebrush, rabbit brush, and juniper trees. The only grass showed up in anemic little clumps, the blades thin and wispy and barely-green.

The sky above me was a thin, pale gray but the light seemed hard and glaring in spite of the cloud cover. Maybe that was the altitude. We were up at 3,000 feet or so. Not especially high, but higher than I was used to. No pun intended.

Maybe some people thought the area was beautiful. That's what I'd heard, anyway. To me it looked almost too familiar, the parched hills so similar to other hills all over the dried-out West. Unforgiving, unsympathetic, fuck-you hills whose only question for you is why you thought it would be a good idea to stop here in such a shitty environment.

House parties are supposed to be non-stop raucous fun, at least among those people I used to hang with. I wasn't having any fun and I needed to decide what to do about that.

I stood in my shirtsleeves on the flagstone patio of my host's rented vacation house and stared at the thin dusting of early November snow draped over the arid landscape. My breath made white clouds in the air in front of me. I should have been cold but I couldn't really feel it. Too wasted.

Jer would have been proud. Here I was, getting higher than the space shuttle, hanging out with a bunch of people I didn't even like, in classic Jeremy Lindstrom style. Party on, dude.

For somebody stoned out of his mind, I was feeling remarkably bitter. Jeremy's death had left me like that. I couldn't get past the fact he'd left me. I couldn't get past the fact I hadn't saved him. I'd let him go, let him drink and drug himself to death and if I were honest with myself I'd helped him on his way.

Blaming his death on the devil was a sad cop-out. The fact was, I was responsible.

There were times I'd loaned him some shit from my own stash when I should have withheld it. Times when I should have found something else for us to do. But I'd been too busy doing my own partying to pay enough attention to Jer's problems.

Yeah, I had tried, along with some of his other friends, to intervene. But none of us had tried hard enough. Especially me. I was his partner in crime, so how hard was I going to push him to stop? Now he was gone and I knew it was my fault.

Maybe it was my fate to hurt anyone who got close to me. Jeremy had been the first, but that was probably because I was only now really getting established as a star. *He* had told my mother he would only take me—or those near me—when I was at the height of my fame.

I liked to think I had more fame, more work in me, but maybe not. Maybe this was it, and now I had to pay the price for my success. Or my friends did, at any rate. Others would probably follow Jeremy. And how was I dealing with his death-by-partying? By partying some more. Drinking and doping were the only ways I could seem to forget.

Why should innocent bystanders have to pay for my dumbshit mistake? It hadn't even been my decision. It was my mom's. Why should Jeremy die because she was too ambitious for her own good?

Why couldn't I forget this shit no matter how much crap I dumped into my body?

Maybe it was because ever since Jeremy's death, that *thing* had followed me around. It would turn up at odd moments, invading my sense of solitude, ruining my peace of mind. What little peace of mind I had, at any rate.

I could sense it now. Watching me.

I snorted. Whatever. It wouldn't find anyone to kill here, as long as it was only picking on people I cared about. No-one here fit that description. Not even me.

Maybe, just maybe, that was the real reason behind all the current partying. Avoidance. These were people I didn't care for, people who weren't really my friends. They were safe. As long as I stayed wasted, stayed with people who didn't matter to me, nobody would get hurt.

Behind me in the sprawling contemporary house, music thumped and people whooped with laughter. I wasn't feeling it. I'd had all the fun at this party that I could stand.

The sliding glass door slid open and a girl tottered out on heels so high they could double as stilts. Her skirt was so short every time she bent over you could see her pussy. She wasn't wearing any panties. I knew all this because all yesterday and last night, she'd made sure to bend over as often as she could manage, usually pointing her ass at me when she did it.

Her name was Violet something-or-other, a model and aspiring actress with five pounds of make-up and fake eyelashes that would have looked more realistic on a giraffe. She batted them at me and leaned on my arm, licking her glossy upper lip as a cloud of her perfume rose up to choke me.

"Hey, Gage. What're you doing out here all by yourself?"

"Getting some fresh air." Getting away from her pussy displays.

She was only one of many women who'd been throwing themselves at me ever since I'd arrived. A couple of years ago, I'd have been all over that. Now I just wanted to get the hell away.

Something in me had broken when Jeremy died. This shit wasn't fun anymore. So what was I doing here? Why was I hanging around with a bunch of assholes I didn't like, didn't even really know, didn't want to know? There had to be something better than this.

Jeremy was gone, and...fuck. The only person in my life who really meant anything to me was my mother. I didn't have any real friends. Not these assholes, for sure. You know something is severely wrong with your life when your only friends are people you can't stand.

It was safer for everyone if I kept away from people I could truly care about. Kept myself distant from everyone, relating only through booze and drugs. Sometimes, though, the emptiness of this shit just got to me and I couldn't take it anymore.

All at once, the only thing I could think about was getting away. Going somewhere I could be alone—really alone. Somewhere people weren't totally wrapped up in their next high.

"We missed you in there." Violet pressed her abundant, possibly fake, tits against my arm.

I didn't say anything. It was around noon, I guessed, although I wasn't sure. I'd been up since some time the day before and my sense of time was hazy. But if I left now, I should be able to make it back to the Willamette Valley before dark. Maybe.

It was worth a try, because I didn't think I could stand spending another night with this crowd. I could hole up in a hotel for a day or two before catching a flight back to L.A.

"Come back inside. I'll show you my room." Violet grabbed my crotch.

"Jesus, Violet." I shoved her hand away.

She pouted. It wasn't attractive. "Everybody said you like to have a good time. They said you're fun. But you've been totally boring all weekend."

"I am completely and utterly boring," I said.

"Let me show you how to have a good time." She went for the crotch again.

"No, thanks. Maybe some other time." I swiveled and made for the house.

Pot smoke filled the air of the huge living room. There was a cloud of it clinging to the thick wooden beams of the cathedral ceiling, and that was the mildest of the substances people were passing around. Two guys and a couple of girls were doing lines of coke laid out on the chunky stone coffee table, and someone in the corner was shooting H into his femoral artery. He had his jeans down around his knees and didn't give a shit who was watching.

I couldn't feel the bitterness anymore. A weird sense of detachment had come over me, like I was somewhere outside of the scene instead of in it. My body felt far away, my consciousness sort of floating over my own head.

It wasn't just the drugs. At least, I didn't think so. There was something else going on, some shift in my mind.

Everyone in the room, including me, looked hollow. Not because I could see inside them, but because they didn't seem to have anything inside. They were emptier and flimsier than cracker boxes with all the crackers gone.

Most of them had known Jer, at least a little. Had they forgotten him already? Didn't they remember how he'd died? But it didn't matter to them. The only thing they cared about was getting their next fix.

Violet tottered after me as I walked my hollow ass through the drug-addled crowd in the living room. She was chattering about giving me the time of my life. I ignored her, heading for the bedrooms.

They'd given me my own room, but when I got there I found a guy and two girls, a blonde and a brunette, in the middle of my king-sized bed. Naked. They made a kind of erotic pretzel, all twined together.

My detachment vanished in an instant, replaced by rage.

Two naked females twined together was the kind of sight that would once have turned me on. Now it just made me fucking furious. They were in my private room, for fuck's sake.

One of the girls lifted her bleached blond head and smiled, her eyes glazed and unfocused. She was definitely on something. "Hey, Gage. Wanna join us?"

"No. Get out of my room."

The guy glared at me over his shoulder. "We're in the middle of something here."

"Get the fuck out of my room."

He buried his head between the brunette's thighs, making her giggle loudly. I growled and kicked the bed frame.

"What's your fucking problem, bro?" the guy snarled.

"You're not my bro. Now get out of my room!" I gave the bed another kick for emphasis.

"Jesus. All right. Just chill out." He levered himself off the bed. "Come on, girls. We'll find another room."

I glowered at them until they'd hauled their naked asses off my bed and exited the room. Guess I could've packed up while they were getting each other off, but it was the principle of the thing. They had no business taking over my room for their fuck party.

I grabbed my overnight bag from the closet floor and started stuffing laundry in it. Most of my shit was still in the bag because I hadn't bothered unpacking. It made for a nice, quick exit.

"Gage?" Violet minced over to me and got down on her knees in front of me, reaching up to stroke my dick through my jeans.

I flinched back. "Knock it off."

"But don't you want me to? I'd love to make you feel good."

"Violet, do us both a favor and get away from me. I'm not in the mood for this today."

She pouted again. Maybe she thought it looked seductive. It didn't.

"I'm starting to think you don't like me," she whined, clambering awkwardly to her feet.

Bingo.

I carried my bag into the bathroom. "Just having a bad day."

"But I could make it better."

She could never make anything better. Not for me. There was zero chance of *him* taking Violet.

"Vi, I'm trying to be patient, but I'm running out. Don't push me or you're going to see a side of me you won't like." I shoveled my shaving kit stuff into my bag loose, letting the shaving cream and razor and toothbrush and all the other related junk land randomly on top of the wads of dirty clothes inside.

"Where are you going?" she said.

"Away." I stalked past her, through the bedroom and into the hallway.

Nobody else seemed to notice when I walked out the front door. My bodyguards were probably in the kitchen, where they'd hung out for most of this party. They didn't see me leave and I wasn't about to tell them I was going. I wanted to be alone.

I'd rented a red Porsche. It was sitting off to the side of the driveway at the end so I wouldn't get blocked in by all the other guests.

Driving high as I was could not be a good idea. Oh fucking well. I was going, high or not. I tossed my bag in the back and slid into the driver's side. Just as I shut my door, Violet staggered out of the house.

"Jesus," I muttered, gunning the engine.

I backed out and peeled off without acknowledging her. It was best not to encourage her. She'd probably try to invite herself into the car with me, and I didn't think I could take several hours trapped in a sports car with Violet. One of us would end up dead.

Chapter 5
The Road

I needed not only to get away from that crappy house party but to get somewhere I could spend the night. No way did I want to sleep all crammed into the Porsche, so I needed to make good time and get my ass into Eugene, the little Willamette Valley town which had the closest real airport.

The highway climbed rapidly into the Cascades and with the change in elevation the landscape became wetter and greener. When I crossed the pass and descended the western slopes of the range, the air went from dry enough to desiccate the inside of your nasal passages to moist and fragrant with the scent of the forest. I'd entered another world where evergreen trees so dark they were almost black pressed thickly against the edges of the road and underbrush—ferns, grass, bushes I couldn't identify—completely hid the ground.

A gloomy forest that even the bright whiteness of the new snow couldn't lighten. In my ugly mood, the terrain seemed ominous. Haunted.

It went right along with the haunted atmosphere inside the car. You wouldn't think a Porsche could feel that way, would you? Well, it can. Something invisible had hitched a ride in my passenger seat. And I didn't know how to kick it out.

I snagged the bottle of Scotch from the passenger seat—it was sitting on my invisible guest's lap—and tipped it to my mouth. Yeah, I know. Drinking and driving. All I can say is my brain was partially off-line due to lack of sleep and all the shit I'd already put in my body.

I was making one stupid decision after another.

The booze put a warm glow back into me, a mellow haze that further distorted my thinking. I felt looser, more relaxed, not so pissed off about the party. The Porsche swooped around the curves of the road like a bright red bird, and in my mind I was flying. When I hit a patch of ice and spun sideways, I just threw back my head and laughed. The green-black forest whirled around me as my car did a one-eighty in the middle of the highway.

I was lucky there weren't any other cars on the road that day.

I pointed the car in the right direction again and drove off, a bit more slowly. Didn't want to end up at the bottom of a cliff, after all. Even if my haunting friend wished I would.

Fuck him. I wasn't going to make this easy for him.

My stomach started to ache. Normally I don't get stomach pain with alcohol unless I drink myself into oblivion, and I wasn't that drunk. Maybe I was just hungry. There weren't many places to stop for food on this lonely mountain road, though, and I hadn't brought anything with me.

A few flakes whirled out of the sky and hit my windshield. Then a few more. They grew fatter, faster, closer together. The Porsche had no snow tires, but that was okay. I was a good driver and I felt fine except for the nausea building in my stomach.

I really needed to stop somewhere and get something to eat.

Up ahead and to my right was a big wooden sign directing me to Mountain Magic Lodge and Cabins. Painfully corny name, but they'd have food at a lodge, right? I swerved into the narrow drive, the car fishtailing as I headed down a steep hill.

The car slid all the way down the slope and into a smallish parking lot, where it performed a gentle one-eighty. An empty parking lot. The log-cabin style lodge, which turned out to be kind of small and run down, looked empty too, its windows dark. A handful of shabby cottages clustered around it like they were huddling in for shelter.

I cut the engine and got out of the car, swinging the Scotch bottle by its neck. A thin layer of unbroken snow, marred only by my tire tracks, covered the lot. Nobody had been here for a few days at least.

Crunching through the fresh snow, I wandered across the open lot and around the side of the lodge building with the vague idea that someone might be hanging out in the back. All I found back there was a sad little concrete patio that overlooked a gray and angry looking river. There wasn't a lot of space between the patio and the river, which made me wonder how often it flooded in the spring.

The patio, I mean. Did the river water rise high enough to flood that postage-stamp patio?

It wasn't flooded at the moment, though, and I had a drunken desire to get a closer look at the water. Plus my bladder was yelling at me to take a piss and I didn't want to make yellow snow right here at the back door of the lodge. That would be in serious bad taste.

I took another slug of Scotch before wending my way through some stiff evergreen ferns to the water's edge. Boy, that water looked cold and fast. It would probably get a lot higher before summer came.

The invisible guest watched me from some distance away. Don't ask me how I knew this. I could feel it. *He* was somewhere behind me, not too close, not within reaching distance. Just watching. I would have flipped him off, but pissing seemed more important at the moment.

I started unbuttoning my jeans, but I fumbled, my fingers refusing to cooperate. For some reason, they seemed kind of stiff and uncooperative. Or maybe they were too loose. I couldn't make up my mind.

Either way, they couldn't seem to get a grip on my pants.

I stared down at the metal button for a moment, looking at it through the white clouds of my breath. It seemed strangely far away for the waistband button of a pair of jeans. Almost like it belonged to someone else. The ground beneath my feet seemed to waver and slide away from me, tilting unpredictably. No wonder I couldn't get my pants open, with the ground moving like that.

Carefully I bent down and set the bottle in the snow. My vision gave this weird lurch, as if the whole world had tried to up-end itself. I straightened even more carefully, trying to keep the dizziness under control, and wrestled the button out of its hole. Good job. Now the zipper. Zippers were easy. No prob. Just a straight shot down the fly.

I shifted my weight. Something about the movement made me pitch forward. I flailed, throwing my arms out to catch myself. But the ground under my feet gave way, sliding down and forward into the water. My hand slapped against the icy trunk of a young tree and slid, scraping my palm without giving me any purchase.

Fuck.

I had only an instant to register what was happening. The water hit me like a blow, the cold stealing my breath. It closed over my head.

I bobbed up again, broke the surface, tried to get a look at the bank. All I could see was tossing gray water, spinning gray sky. I captured a lung full of air and then the water swallowed me again.

Something slammed into my skull. The shock reverberated all the way down my spine. Everything went black and I disappeared.

Chapter 6

The River

Nova:

The cabin smelled like woodsmoke. My cookstove burned wood and looked like it belonged in the nineteenth century, which I'd always thought was awesome. I was still learning to cook on the thing, but I'd made a lot of progress.

It kept the kitchen almost too hot at times. Right now, though, it felt just about right.

The mountains can be cold even in early November. Luckily, my parents' cabin was well-built, not just sturdy with a snow-worthy roof but chinked up tight so it wasn't drafty in the winter. With the wood-burning cookstove, I was completely cozy so far, and I had a second stove in the living room in case the weather got truly dire.

Winter was here already. I glanced out the cabin window and confirmed that—yep—it was really snowing. Most of the stuff falling from the dull gray sky was rain, but there were snowflakes sprinkled in for a bit of variety.

What did they call that stuff? Sleet, I thought. Snow mixed with rain.

We'd had some snow already, but most of it hadn't stuck. It melted as soon as it hit the ground, or maybe lasted overnight and disappeared by noon the next day. Only an inch or so had stuck around so far. But I had a feeling this stuff was going to be here for a while. Good thing I had plenty of well-seasoned firewood to last me through the winter.

Speaking of, I needed to make a quick trip to the woodpile.

A few minutes later, I'd put on a scarf and gloves and a hat to keep the sleet out of my eyes. I didn't have any fancy carriers for the wood, so there would be multiple trips to and from the woodpile before I'd stocked up the house.

I opened the back door. A man stood there, watching the door as if he were waiting for me. I jumped, stumbling back a step.

He was tall and skinny. He wore a flannel shirt but no jacket and no hat. His dark blond hair was long and lank, but it wasn't stuck to his head with wet, so he couldn't have been outside for very long.

"I'm sorry if I scared you," he said, his voice pleasant and respectful. "I need your help."

This was weird. I lived on a narrow side road that wasn't especially easy to see from the highway. It wasn't the kind of place people found by accident, so how had he ended up here?

I narrowed my eyes suspiciously. "What for?"

"My friend fell in the river. I need your help to pull him out." He pointed through the trees toward the McKenzie.

"I'm not that strong," I said. "Maybe I should call someone to help you."

"A call would be a good idea," he said. "But you need to go down and pull him out right now. He's almost gone."

I didn't know whether to believe him or not. It could be some kind of trick designed to get me to let down my guard. Maybe draw me away from the house for whatever nefarious plan he might have. On the other hand, what if his friend really had fallen in the water? In this weather, he'd only have a few minutes before hypothermia killed him.

"I'll be right back," I said to the blond.

Shutting the door on him, I locked it and went for the pistol my dad had given me. From now on, I was wearing it in the waistband of my pants. Just in case. I'd carry it openly at the moment, though, so Mystery Man knew he couldn't screw with me.

Armed, I reopened the door. The blond guy was standing right where I'd left him, like he hadn't moved a quarter inch. He glanced at the gun in my hand, but said nothing. All he did was turn on his heel and walk toward the river.

The water was already high, even though it was early in the season, not even officially winter yet. We'd had an extremely wet fall this year. The river, sweetly refreshing in the summer, seemed resentful now as it bullied its way through stands of pussy willow, wild currant, and salmonberry that were high and dry in June.

The blond pointed toward the water. "There he is. See him?"

I peered through naked branches. There was something floating in the water, some large and bright red object that seemed to be caught on a partially submerged sapling. I wouldn't have picked it out as a human form if this guy hadn't told me it was his friend. From here, it looked like a vague lump that could just as easily have been a chunk of garbage someone had tossed into the current so they wouldn't have to pay to take it to a dump.

But as I drew closer, I could see it wasn't garbage. It was a man.

He floated face up in the gray current, his dark brown hair swirling restlessly in the restless water. His skin looked so pale it was almost blue, and that made me shiver. There was something unreal about the sight of him, like it belonged in a movie instead of my boring real life.

He wore a red jacket and blue jeans. How long had he been in the water? He might be dead already.

My guide had dropped back as I got closer to the bank. I turned to ask him how his friend had fallen in, but he was gone.

"Hey!" I yelled. "Aren't you going to help me get him out?"

The only answer I got was the barely audible shushing sound of the increasingly thick snowfall. Where had the guy gone? I couldn't even see his tracks in the snow, although mine were clear. My whole scalp prickled as I stared around myself in bafflement. He couldn't have simply disappeared.

Yet that seemed to be exactly what he'd done.

I checked the safety to make sure it was on and stuck my pistol into my coat pocket. Wherever he'd gone, I still had his nearly drowned friend on my hands and no-one to help me rescue him. Taking a deep breath, I plunged into the icy water of the river.

Holy hell, it was cold. The kind of cold that stops your lungs and sends a burning ache right into your bones. I gritted my teeth and waded through the thigh-deep water toward the man.

His right sleeve had caught on a branch of that partly drowned sapling, and that was what had saved him from being drawn back out into the main current. Instead he was floating in this tiny backwater behind my cabin, looking almost peaceful, his features starkly beautiful, like those of a statue. Or maybe he just looked dead.

I swallowed heavily as I reached for him. If he was dead, it would be the first time I'd ever touched a corpse. I probably would have been a lot more scared if it weren't for the unbelievable cold of the river and the urgent hope that I could save this guy I'd never seen before.

My hand met his face. It was almost as cold as the water. I didn't have time to check for a pulse, so I grabbed his arm and tried to yank the sleeve free of the branch that had taken it hostage. The thin fabric of his jacket tore. His body began to drift out toward the center of the river.

"Shit! Don't do that," I said. As if he could hear me.

I grabbed his arm with both hands and pulled him toward the bank, leaning and using all the strength in my body to guide him against the force of the current. And praying all the while that he was still alive and I wasn't dragging a corpse.

We reached the shallow water at the bank's edge and I walked backward onto solid ground. My body instantly felt about a hundred pounds heavier without the buoyancy of the water. How was I going to get this guy, who looked to be at least six feet tall, up the slope to the cabin?

In a desperate burst of energy, I hauled him out of the river. He lay on the muddy snow of the bank with his face up to the falling flakes, which settled on his pale skin and melted. At least they weren't sticking. Didn't that mean his skin still had a little warmth in it? Or maybe it was only the river water clinging to him that was melting the snow.

I pressed my fingers lightly to the side of his neck, trying to find a pulse from his carotid artery. There it was, faint and frighteningly slow, but steady. He was still alive.

On the other hand, he was soaked through with the coldest water I'd ever experienced and it was starting to snow heavily, the rain completely replaced with flakes. We were both soaked. If I couldn't get him inside, he wouldn't last more than a few minutes and neither would I.

I grabbed him under the armpits and pulled him backwards up the slope. But I'd already worn myself out hauling him out of the river, and he was way heavier now he didn't have the water to hold him up. I heaved and pulled and made it about a foot and a half before I had to stop. My arms were trembling with the effort.

"Shit," I muttered. "Now what?"

I couldn't leave him out here to die. But he wouldn't survive if I didn't get him dry and warm, pronto. And how could I do that out here? In a few minutes we were both going to be covered in snow. If only I had a tent.

Wait...a tent. There was an old one in the closet of the cabin. I saw it when I cleaned up after I first moved in. It might have holes in it, but it would be better than nothing. Maybe if I could keep the snow off us, I could warm him up enough that he'd awake and walk to the cabin on his own.

"I'll be right back," I said to Mr. Unconscious. "Don't go anywhere."

He didn't even flicker an eyelash. I staggered up the hill to the cabin and raced to the storage closet. There were piles of old junk inside, accumulated over years of family summers up here. Inflatable pool toys, long deflated; extra kerosene lanterns; a box of fishing tackle, along with a rod and reel hiding in the back corner; and at the bottom on the floor, two tattered sleeping bags and an equally disreputable tent.

Awesome. We were going to stay in deluxe accommodations.

I threw a couple of logs on the fire in my woodburning kitchen stove to keep it going while I was outside with The Guy. Then I gathered up the things, somehow holding both sleeping bags and the tent all at once, and staggered back outside. The icy winter air cut right through my wet clothes, making me shiver. It was even worse than being immersed in the river. My jeans stuck to my legs and my feet squished in my sodden shoes. I was going to turn into a Nova-shaped icicle in a minute.

The guy in the red jacket was much worse off. He hadn't moved at all since I'd left him. He really looked dead. His lips were blue, his face and fingers so pale they also looked bluish.

For the first time since coming up here, I wished I wasn't alone. If I'd had a companion, I could have done more for this guy and done it quicker. As it was, I had to fumble around on my own and everything seemed to take ten times longer than it should.

I set the sleeping bags under the canopy of a young spruce tree to keep them out of the snow. Then I untied the tent bundle. What unfurled wasn't what I'd hoped for.

I didn't have a nice, big tent with a floor and a zip-up door. What I had was a pup tent and an old blue tarp. But it was better than nothing and at least it was simple enough that I wouldn't get confused and end up tangling us in the tent like fish in a net. I'd never been very good at pitching tents.

Spreading the tarp on the ground next to the unconscious man, I then rolled him over onto it. Now he was face down, so I heaved him onto his back. He groaned and coughed. Water spewed from his mouth.

I'd placed the tarp under the spruce tree next to the sleeping bags, figuring we could use the extra shelter the tree would provide. Now I draped the pup tent over the lowest branch, arranging the fabric so it hung down to the ground on either side of the man. Okay. So far, so good.

But I didn't have him undressed or in the sleeping bags yet.

My shivering had turned violent and my teeth were starting to chatter. I needed to get warm and dry, too. Crawling into the tent, I crouched on my knees beside him and whipped my utility knife out of my belt. I carried that puppy everywhere, all the time out here.

I used the blade—which I kept sharp at all times—to cut his clothing off him. The stuff looked expensive, although it was a little hard to tell when it was full of water. I didn't care if he'd paid thousands of dollars for it. The clothes were coming off.

After I'd sliced through jacket, Henley, jeans and even boxers, I tossed the scraps out of the tent. I grabbed the sleeping bags and dragged them inside. One went beneath the guy for some insulation from the cold of the ground, which was seeping right through the tarp. I spread the other one over him and tucked it in.

Now for my clothes. All this moving around was awkward in the cramped confines of a pup tent. My hat was still dry somehow, but the rest of me was soaked and my fingers were going numb. I undressed quicker than I'd ever thought possible and crawled under the sleeping bag with my anonymous friend.

Okay. Now I was buck naked and pressed up against an equally naked unconscious stranger who felt a lot like a big block of ice. Still shivering, I tucked the sleeping bag around us, trying to seal out all the cold air. The top of the bag came just over our heads. Thank goodness it was extra-large, and seemed to be made of down. It might just save his life.

God, it was cold in here. The only heat available had to come from my body, and I was chilled too. But this was all we had at the moment, so it would have to do.

While I'd been undressing him, I'd been too preoccupied to pay much attention to his looks, but I had noticed with a corner of my mind that he was quite good-looking. Now there wasn't anything left for me to do, and I could study him in detail.

There wasn't much light in our little nest, but I could see the striking planes of his face, the hardness of his jaw beneath the dark stubble growing there, the high sculpted cheekbones, the length and thickness of his lashes. And I could feel the hard muscularity of his body beneath mine.

Boy, could I feel it.

He was like a stone statue under me, cold and hard with sculpted muscles. He must work out a lot. Like it could be his job, judging by how built he was.

His face looked vaguely familiar, but I couldn't place him. Maybe he just reminded me of someone else. That happened to me a lot—I'd see someone I thought I knew and then realize they only resembled my acquaintance. That was probably what I had here.

Besides, if I'd ever met anyone half as good-looking as this guy, I'd definitely remember his name. Compared to him, Barry wasn't even worth a second glance.

The situation was too bizarre, though, and he was too cold for me to get excited at being mashed up against his nakedness. It just didn't feel sexy at all. My body still shook with hard tremors and I was scared that he'd never wake up.

What would I do if I couldn't rouse him? My phone had been in my jeans pocket when I waded into the river and it was just as soaked as the rest of my stuff. I couldn't call for help. I couldn't leave him because he'd succumb to the cold long before I could get back. All I could do was lay here and hope my body heat was enough to bring him back.

"Look, I don't know who you are," I said out loud. "But you've got to hold on. I'm trying to get you warmed up."

Of course he didn't say anything.

"Don't die on me, okay? I want you to live."

Tori Minard

It was like talking to a rock, but I kept babbling, telling him about the cabin and the river and how this was the first serious snow of the fall.

Was it only my imagination, or was it getting a little warmer inside the sleeping bag? I wasn't shivering anymore, although I still felt cold. It seemed we were making progress.

Then he started to shake.

Chapter 7
Cold

Gage:

Cold. I was trapped someplace cold and dark, like a meat locker or a drawer in the morgue. All I could see or feel was cold darkness, everywhere, even inside me. Cold, hard darkness.

My mind drifted between wanting to escape that cold and wishing I could sink back into it and forget everything. At the moment, I was leaning toward the forgetting.

Someone was talking. The voice went on and on, soft and feminine, but I couldn't understand the words. There seemed to be a heavy, clinging fog wrapped around my legs as it tried to drag me back into the icy black. Although I couldn't understand the voice, it pulled me upward, away from the cold and the forgetfulness.

And there was noise beyond the talking. A strange clattering sound, like nothing I'd ever heard before.

My body shook uncontrollably. I tried to hold onto myself, to stop the movements, but my muscles refused to obey. All I could do was lay there and tremble.

A small hand touched my face. Her skin was hot against mine. I noticed the rest of her pressed against me, then, from chest to knees. She lay over me like a blanket. Who was she? I'd never heard that voice before.

God, she felt good. If I didn't feel like absolute shit, I would have been aroused. Highly aroused. I knew this, but it was an abstraction, an idea. True arousal was out of my reach.

I groaned. The clattering sound paused for an instant before resuming.

The woman gasped. "Are you awake? Can you hear me?"

My mouth wouldn't work, wouldn't form words, so I groaned again. And once again, the clattering stopped. Then started.

My teeth. That sound was my teeth chattering.

"Can you open your eyes?" she said.

Jesus. I just wanted her to shut up so I could go back to sleep. That was what I needed. Sleep. I was so fucking tired. My body felt as heavy as if someone had replaced my blood with lead.

"Open your eyes," she said. "Come on. Please. Open them for me." Her small hands clutched my shoulders and shook me.

"Leave me alone," I muttered. But it came out sounding all mashed together, like one long, unintelligible word.

"Wake up. We can't stay here. You have to wake up." Small hands shook me again, harder this time.

All right. Fine. I'd open my eyes for her.

Yeah. I'd get right on that.

I struggled to pry my eyelids apart. A sliver of light entered my eyes. Victory. I tried to summon some enthusiasm for my accomplishment, but it was too much trouble. The sliver disappeared.

"Come on," she nagged. "Open your eyes. I know you can do it. We can't stay here. We have to get inside."

What the hell was she talking about? Inside where? I was fine where I was.

Okay, not really. But I sure wasn't getting up and going somewhere else.

A sharp object jabbed me mercilessly in the ribs. "I know you're in there somewhere. I'm not going to give up until you look at me."

Oh, for fuck's sake.

I put everything I had into opening my eyes.

It was dark, but not too dark to see. The light felt gray and cold, just like my body. A girl lay on top of me and neither of us wore any clothes.

I squinted up at her. She had dark hair and eyes, a pretty face with a slightly pointy chin. She reminded me of a small, naked elf. I didn't recognize her. Shouldn't I recognize her, given we were naked and horizontal together? We must have done something intimate to be in that condition.

But if we'd been screwing, why did I feel so bad?

I was still shaking, my teeth rattling together. The exhaustion weighed on me, making it difficult to keep my eyes open. Yet I wanted to stare at her. She was more than pretty—her features were beautiful and completely free of make-up, which also puzzled me. The girls I knew wore tons of make-up at all times.

She gave me a dazzling smile. "You did it! You're awake."

I groaned incoherently in response.

"Now we just have to get you on your feet."

Another groan escaped me. "Nah."

I'd meant to say "not gonna happen" but apparently that was too much work for me at the moment.

"We have to. It's getting colder. It's snowing like crazy. We have to get inside where it's warm."

I kept squinting at her, trying to make sense of her words. We were outside? In a snowstorm. What the fuck, over?

"Come on," she said, rolling off me.

I immediately missed her heat and the softness of her curves. But she was on a mission and there was no stopping her. She got on her knees and pulled the coverings off me. A sleeping bag. I got a flash of a voluptuous body just before she wrapped the puffy bag around herself.

"You can use the one you're lying on," she said.

I just lay there staring at her.

She frowned and extended a hand. "Do you need help getting up?"

In other circumstances, that remark would have made me grin wickedly. But grinning would take energy I didn't have. Instead I continued to stare like a fool.

"Look," she said, her voice growing sharp. "I know you feel terrible, but we can't stay here. You're still cold. You could die out here, and I won't let that happen. So get up right now. The cabin is really close. I know you can walk that far."

She was stubborn as hell.

I struggled to get myself propped up on my elbows. No idea where I was, who she was, or how and why I'd come to be here, but I decided getting into a warm cabin sounded like a fine plan.

"Clothes," I said hoarsely.

In spite of the dim light, her blush was obvious. "Um ... I had to cut them off you. But I have your shoes." She reached outside the tent.

There was a tent?

God, my head was a mess. I'd just noticed the fact we were inside some kind of tiny tent with a steep pitch that gave just enough room for the two of us. Glancing up, I saw that the fabric was draped over the branch of an evergreen tree. Its prickly green needles were just above my head.

She handed me my shoes. They were liberally dusted with snow. She wanted me to put my feet in those?

"It's better than going barefoot," she said, tapping the snow out of them.

They were fucking cold when I put them on, and completely wet, like they'd been dunked in an ice bath. She helped me wrap up in the remaining sleeping bag and we crawled out of the tent, me staggering like a drunk even though I was on my hands and knees. Walking in this state was going to be lots of fun.

Sure enough, it was snowing like crazy outside. The flakes were so thick and came down so fast, so heavily, it was like trying to look through a curtain. All I could see was blurry shapes that looked like trees. A lot of trees.

A rushing sound, like a busy freeway, came from nearby.

The girl grabbed me around my ribs and hauled me to my feet. She was stronger than she looked. And I was weak as a newborn puppy, swaying and wobbling as dizziness made everything spin around me.

"It's real close," she said.

That was a lie.

It seemed to take years of stumbling through the freezing snowfall to get to the cabin. All my effort, all my mental focus went to putting one foot ahead of the other and staying upright. Finally, a rough brown wall reared up in front of us, along with a short flight of wooden stairs to a tiny deck.

"Just three steps," she said.

I was so tired; I just wanted to sit down on those snow-covered steps and rest. But I had her nagging me, tugging on me, and it was easier to go along with what she wanted.

Chapter 8

Unexpected Guest

Nova:

My guest sprawled limply in one of my kitchen chairs, his head lolling to the side, supported by the rough log wall of the cabin. His eyelids remained at half-mast, his gaze unfocused and vague. Water dripped off him and pooled on the old, multi-colored vinyl floor.

He was so heavy that by the time I got him into the chair, my legs and arms were shaking. The guy was six-plus feet of muscle and bone. Mostly muscle. But he was weak from hypothermia and maybe other things, and he couldn't walk steadily. He kept weaving and swaying like he was drunk.

Maybe he was. Maybe that was why he'd fallen into the river in the first place.

If so, he was damn lucky to be alive.

I had to get him warmed up, both the outside of him and the inside. He needed to get completely dry and he had to drink some warm liquid to get the heat inside his body. But I needed to get warm and dry, too, or I wouldn't be able to take care of him.

I left him in the kitchen while I climbed into my loft bedroom for some dry clothes. The fire had burned down quite a bit while I was outside with him, so when I returned to the kitchen, I built it up again and put a pan of water on to heat for tea. He just sat there staring off into space, blinking every so often but mainly looking completely out of it.

"I'm going back out for your stuff," I said, sticking my feet into my warmest boots.

He turned his head and blinked at me, his face expressionless. Damn, he was gorgeous.

How had I failed to see it before? I guess I'd been too busy trying to save him. He had high cheekbones and a squarish jaw with a dimple in his chin. I never used to like those, but on him it was charming. Sexy.

His eyes were huge, thick-lashed and bright blue, and his lips...holy hell, he had the most kissable looking lips I'd ever seen. They weren't especially full, but they weren't thin, either. They were perfectly sized and had this beautifully curved, sculpted shape that made me want to trace their edges with my fingertip.

Unfortunately, those gorgeous eyes of his were blank. It was like he didn't know where he was, or maybe even *who* he was. The idea disturbed me. I hoped he didn't have amnesia.

"Uh...so, like I said, I'm going to get your stuff. I'll be right back."

He just stared at me.

Okay, then. I dashed outside, pulling the hood of my coat up over my wet hair. The snow had deepened in the short time we'd been inside and it was starting to drag the tent down. I snatched up his half-frozen gear and dashed back to the cabin, shutting the door with a sigh of relief.

Then I remembered—oh, shit—I'd never gotten around to bringing in the firewood. But I had enough to last me another few hours, and I had to get some hot liquid into my unexpected guest first.

The kitchen felt almost hot after the miserable cold of that tent. He slumped in the chair, leaning against the log wall, his eyes closed, the damp sleeping bag still wrapped around him. I shucked my coat, draped it on one of the other chairs, and laid my hand against his forehead. His skin still felt cold to the touch.

Should I wake him up again? I wasn't sure how to handle this situation. What would my parents do?

They'd probably check him for concussion, for one thing. Then, of course, they'd try to get as much hot liquid into him as possible, and for that he had to be awake.

I bent over him and gently lifted an eyelid. Beautiful, beautiful eyelid fringed with lashes so long and thick they didn't even look real. His gorgeousness was a dangerous distraction.

The pupil of that eye looked normal and so did the other one. He could still have a concussion, but at least he didn't seem to have any severe symptoms. The confusion and wobbliness could be due to hypothermia.

I just wished I'd had the common sense to keep my phone from getting wet and ruined. A helicopter flight to the emergency room in Eugene would make me feel a lot better about his chances.

For now, I had to get him as warm and dry as possible. In the master bedroom, I found some extra blankets. I took them to the kitchen and placed them on the table. His eyes were still closed. His lips looked less blue, though, so he seemed to be improving.

I tugged at the sleeping bag, damp from the water all over his body. He lifted his lids and gazed dully at me.

"Let's get this wet thing off you," I said. "Stand up for a sec."

After another moment of dull staring, he seemed to comprehend what I'd said enough to get onto his feet. I whipped the sleeping bag off him, keeping my gaze away from his nakedness.

That took all the mental strength I had, because the temptation to stare at all that male gorgeousness was overwhelming. But it was also kinda creepy, given that he was so out of it he didn't seem to really know what I was doing.

I threw one of the extra blankets around him before he sank back into the chair. Then I wrapped a second one around his back and over his head. He looked like a disaster survivor, which I suppose he was, in a way. His own personal disaster.

I leaned down and smiled at him. "I'm Nova, by the way. What's your name?"

His eyes narrowed, like he was struggling to remember. "Gay."

His name was Gay? That seemed unlikely, but okay, I was going with it.

"Um...well, it's nice to meet you, Gay," I said, on my best polite behavior. "I'm going to get you warmed up, okay?"

He just blinked a few times and closed his eyes again.

My water was boiling. I poured some over a couple bags of decaf tea, one in each giant mug. I needed heat, too. But when I turned around, "Gay" was pulling off the blankets and dropping them on the floor, leaving his delectable body utterly bare.

"Hey," I said, trying not to look too closely. "Don't do that. You need them."

"Hot," he said.

"You're not hot. You need the blankets." I bent down and scooped them into my arms.

"Too hot."

"No," I said, draping one of the blankets around him again. Still not looking. "Your core body temperature is dangerously low. You need this."

He batted at my hand. "Too hot. Leave."

"You only think you're too hot. The hypothermia is confusing you."

He certainly looked confused, his gaze muddled. He was too big for me to successfully fight, if it came down to that. But I wrapped the second blanket around him anyway.

"It would make me really happy if you kept those on," I said. "I don't want you to die on me. Okay, Gay? Can you do that for me?"

"Gay?" He looked even more confused than before.

"Yeah. You told me your name is Gay."

"No. Gage." He drew out the second word, as if to make sure I understood.

"Gage?" I repeated.

He nodded, then winced and closed his eyes. "Fuck."

"You have a headache?"

"Yeah," he said, his voice so low it was hard to hear.

"Are you dizzy?"

"Yeah."

"That's because you got so cold. You need to warm up. I know you feel hot right now, but your brain is playing a trick on you. We still need to get you warmer."

I wasn't sure if he understood me or if he was even listening. But he settled down and quit trying to undress himself, so I went back to making tea. I stirred in a lot of sugar before bringing his mug to him.

"Gage, you've got to drink this."

He made an incoherent noise in his throat.

"I know you don't want to, but you have to." I held the mug to his beautiful lips. "Come on. Just one sip."

Finally he relented and I got a few drops into him. I took a swallow of my own tea before returning to coaxing him. We continued that way until I'd gotten the whole mug of tea down his throat.

As I made second mugs of tea, it occurred to me that I was now alone in my cabin with a large, unknown male. At the moment, he wasn't in any shape to hurt me. But what about when he felt better? I had no idea who this guy was, and his amazing good looks didn't mean he wasn't some kind of psycho.

Plus, what about the other guy, the blond who'd disappeared on me? That whole episode was so weird it still gave me the creeps. And Blondie was somehow connected to the man sitting in my kitchen.

But what was I going to do? I couldn't in good conscience toss him out into the snow to die. He hadn't done anything...yet...to deserve that.

I still had the pistol. Wait. No, I didn't. It was out in the snow, along with my now-frozen clothes. Well, I'd go get it soon, right before I brought in more firewood.

I set the new mugs of tea on the table. Gage opened his eyes and stared at me.

"Where am I?" he said, his voice slurred.

"You're in my cabin."

"Who are you?"

I frowned. He didn't remember my name? "I'm Nova. Nova Pennyman."

"Nova," he said slowly. "I'm Gage."

"Yeah, I know. You already told me."

Straight, dark brows lowered. "I did?"

"Uh huh." I tried to cover my worry with a friendly smile. "Have some more tea. You're still cold inside."

His frown deepened. "I feel hot."

His hand came up to shove at the blankets. I reached out and grabbed his wrist and a jolt of arousal shot through me. For crying out loud, I was getting turned on by him and he couldn't even remember my name.

"Leave them on," I said. "You feel hot, but inside you're cold. You need to keep on warming up."

He muttered something under his breath.

I gave him his tea. "Drink this. Can you hold the mug?"

He glared at me. "Of course I can."

This time I hid my smile. Maybe he was starting to feel better. At least he was well enough to argue with me.

On the other hand, he'd been uncooperative in the tent. Maybe he was like this all the time.

He reached with shaky hands for the tea mug and lifted it slowly to his mouth. Some of it sloshed over the side, but I kept my hands to myself despite my urge to rescue him. I wouldn't want to insult his masculine pride by babying him.

"How did I get here?" he said, his words still slurred.

"You fell in the river. I pulled you out." I didn't think it was a good time to tell him about his disappearing friend who'd come to me for help.

"River?" he said blankly.

"Yeah. The McKenzie River. You were floating in it. You probably would have died if you'd been in any longer."

He just stared at his mug of tea as if it would reveal the answers to him, solve the puzzle of how he'd ended up in the water.

I didn't want to baby Gage and yet I wanted to take care of him—mainly because I felt like I'd be responsible for his death if I didn't. I've always been kind of over-responsible that way. If someone is in trouble and I don't help and something bad happens to that person, it's partly my fault because I didn't do everything I could. It was that kind of thinking that kept me dribbling tea and later hot soup into Gage's mouth. It was that kind of thinking that had me supporting him as he wobbled his way into the master bedroom to lay down. It was that kind of thinking that got me up twice during the night to check on him and make sure he was still breathing.

Chapter 9
Celebrity

When the sun rose, it brought only pale, weak light filtered through the white of the unrelenting snow. I watched the flakes swirling crazily out of the sky through a gap in my bedroom curtains. This storm was shaping up to be epic.

I was cranky from lack of sleep and sore from all the extra physical work I'd done the day before. And now I had another day of heavy work ahead of me, making sure Gage not only didn't die but recovered fully. I crawled out of my loft and went to build up the fire. The cabin had gotten pretty cold during the night, and that wasn't good for Gage.

Once I had the stove going and some water heating on top, I went back to the master bedroom to check on him. He was on his side, one arm pillowing his head, the covers down around his hips. He had the finest body I'd ever seen, at least in real life. It was the kind of body that a girl like me normally only saw on TV or the movies. Or maybe in an underwear ad.

It was wrong of me to stare. Especially when he was asleep and couldn't defend himself. But that didn't stop me from doing it. I stood in the doorway and gaped at him, admiring the heavy curves of his delts and biceps, the tightness of his waist, the narrow line of dark brown hair that trailed from his chest and down his belly to disappear under the blankets. I really wanted to know what the rest of him looked like.

Then he opened his eyes and looked at me and I felt like my body was catching fire. Not from lust. From complete mortification. He'd caught me.

Sleepy blue eyes gazed at me in obvious confusion. He rubbed his face and frowned. "Uh ... good morning."

I smiled at him. "Good morning. Feeling any better?"

The frown deepened. "Better than what?"

I cocked my head. It seemed he'd forgotten everything I'd told him yesterday. "Do you know who I am?"

His tongue emerged to moisten his lips. Oh, God. He really shouldn't do that. It wasn't fair to me.

"I ... don't know," he said slowly. "Did we—"

"No!" My denial came out so quickly that I felt mortified all over again. "No, we didn't. You've been sick, that's all."

"But..." He squinted up at me. "Where am I? Who are you? Why am I here?"

Oh, boy. "I'm Nova Pennyman." How many times would I have to repeat this?

"Nova Pennyman," he said after me, looking utterly mystified.

"Yeah. This is my cabin. I found you floating in the river yesterday afternoon. I pulled you out and brought you here. You were pretty far gone. I've been worried about you."

"River?"

I bit back a sigh of frustration. This was getting old. "The McKenzie River. Cascade Mountains? Oregon?"

Gage merely stared at me as if I were speaking a foreign language. A really obscure one, from some wild corner of the Himalayas, perhaps.

"So you and me—we don't know each other," he said slowly.

"Nope. I never saw you before yesterday."

He sat up in the bed without bothering to cover himself. The blankets pooled around his waist. I fought without success to avoid ogling his naked torso. Curly dark hair covered his broad chest—a very well-developed chest. I had the most idiotic urge to rub my face in it, to lick his skin.

He was easily the most beautiful man I'd ever seen, in pictures or real life, and I could hardly believe I had him in my cabin.

"You're staring at me," he said with a faint smirk.

Damn. He'd caught me, and that look on his face said he knew exactly what I'd been thinking.

Could I just die now? Please? It didn't seem like too much to ask.

I straightened my back and tried to look cool, like I didn't care I'd been caught with my tongue hanging out. "Just—you know—wondering who you are."

The smirk deepened. "Seriously?"

"Um ... yeah. Why? Should I know you?" Maybe we'd been introduced once and I'd forgotten him, although I could not imagine how or why I would forget someone who looked like that.

One muscular shoulder lifted, then dropped. "Lots of people do."

That was a weird answer. "Ooookay. Well, I don't. So, um, who are you?"

He wasn't making a whole lot of sense, if you asked me. Was he trying to say he was some kind of celebrity? Yeah, right. Nobody famous ever came around here. We had ski slopes nearby, but our little village wasn't some kind of well-known, glamorous resort. We mostly got people from other parts of Oregon.

He sounded more coherent this morning, or at least his voice was no longer slurred. But he was behaving really strangely. Maybe there'd been some long-term damage?

"Gage Dalton," he said, raising his brows at me.

I blinked. Then I laughed. "No way."

Gage Dalton was a famous actor. I wasn't really into TV and movies, not because I disliked them but because I'd never had time. My whole adolescence and college life had been dedicated to study, to getting stellar grades so I could get into a prestigious medical school. I'd enrolled in a highly regarded private college in Avery's Crossing, rather than going to Central Willamette State or University of Oregon like so many of my classmates. Everything in my life had been dedicated to the single goal of becoming a doctor like my parents, so I was a bit clueless when it came to popular actors.

But even I had heard of Gage Dalton.

"Come on," I said. "You're not Gage Dalton."

"Yeah. I am." He sounded a little irritated.

"No, you're not. If you're a famous actor, then how come you were floating in the river? Where's your entourage, or whatever you call it?"

"I don't know. I can't remember anything from yesterday."

"Uh huh. Right." That was sure convenient.

He scowled at me. "Just because I don't remember being in the river doesn't mean I've got total amnesia. I'm telling you that I'm Gage Dalton."

"Okay." I raised my hand in mock surrender. "Whatever you say."

He growled. "Where are my jeans?"

That brought the blush back into my cheeks. "They're in the kitchen. But you can't wear them. I had to cut them off you."

"Bring them here."

At his bossy tone, I crossed my arms over my chest. "Excuse me?"

"Bring them here. I'll show you my I.D."

Well, he sure had the attitude of a spoiled brat movie star, whether he was one or not. And I wasn't in the mood to play along.

"I didn't hear the magic word," I said.

His mouth fell open. "The what?"

"The magic word. You know the one."

His mouth closed with a snap as he glared at me. "You are some piece of work."

"I am?" I glared right back. "Listen, Bud, I'm the one who pulled you out of a freezing river. I'm the only reason you're still alive."

We stared at each other. His jaw looked tight enough to crack walnuts. I just looked back, like I wasn't the least bit intimidated by large naked men sitting around in my private space.

42

His gaze wavered and he sighed. "Okay, you're right. Please bring my jeans in here."

I smiled victoriously. "Sure. I'll be right back."

As I left the room, I heard him groan behind me. He'd been nothing but a pain in the ass since I'd first seen him in the water, but whether it was a side-effect of the hypothermia or his normal state of being I couldn't tell.

The scraps of his jeans were laying where I'd left them on one of the kitchen chairs. They were mostly dry. I fetched them back to him and threw them on the bed.

"There you go."

He gave me a jerky nod as he gathered the pieces onto his lap. "Thanks."

"No problem."

Gage—or whoever he really was—reached in the back pocket of the ruined pants and took out a wallet. He threw it at me. "Have a look."

Okay, sure. I could play this game. I opened the wallet and there was his driver's license. A California license.

Um ... oops. It really did say Gage Dalton, and the address was someplace in Santa Monica. Wasn't that where a lot of rich and famous show business people lived? I had a hazy idea that it might be. And this guy ... this guy just might be the real Gage Dalton after all.

My whole body flushed with embarrassed heat. Now I had a large naked movie star sitting in my space. A gorgeous, muscular, super-famous movie star. Yeah, he'd been a movie star before I'd seen his license, but I hadn't believed it and my skepticism had protected me from any kind of star-struck self-consciousness.

I peeked at him. That cocky smirk was back.

"Now do you believe me?" he said.

I tossed the wallet at him. "Yeah. I believe you."

"All right." He shook his head, then winced. "Can't believe you thought I was lying about that."

Whatever. How was I to know he'd been telling the truth?

His eyes were tense, his brows drawn together. He touched his temple with his fingertips, gingerly. Clearly, he still felt terrible. I didn't want to pester him; I was pretty sure he got pestered on almost an hourly basis. I should leave him alone and let him rest.

On the other hand, he might need something. Considering his recent confusion, he might not even know he needed help.

"You still have a headache?" I said. He might be a famous actor, but he was still hurt and I was responsible for him. I wasn't going to let nervousness get in the way of taking care of him.

His gaze turned wary. Slightly puzzled. "Yes. I do."

"I can give you some Tylenol. Do you drink coffee?"

"Yeah." He still looked puzzled, like I wasn't making sense to him.

Did he expect me to fall down and worship at his feet? If so, he was going to be sadly disappointed.

"Are you okay now?" I came a few steps into the room to get a better look at him. "Do you remember who I am?"

Now his brows both raised and pinched together at the same time. "You just told me your name. Nova Pennyman."

"Right." I smiled. At least he was retaining information for a few minutes at a time, which was a major improvement. And he was aware enough to stare at me like I was either an idiot or crazy and he couldn't make up his mind which one it was. "Good. There are some clothes in the dresser if you want to put something on. I'll have breakfast ready in the kitchen in a little while."

Chapter 10
No Fangirl

Gage:

The bedroom had log walls, round and everything. It looked like it belonged on a set. There were blue and white curtains on the window and a blue and white quilt on the bed. Everything seemed homemade.

The air was warm at least. A vague memory of freezing cold and deep darkness flashed through my mind, making me want to shiver. I controlled myself, though. No shivering or any other show of vulnerability in public.

Okay, so a cabin bedroom isn't exactly public, but I didn't know this Nova girl. She was public to me. Anyone not part of my inner circle represented someone who needed to be managed.

My jeans still retained some chilly dampness where the material was extra thick. They felt clammy against my thighs. The wallet she'd thrown at me sat in my hands like a brick, or maybe a bomb.

She had to believe me now, after seeing my I.D. I couldn't stop smirking at her.

My hostess, or whatever she was, turned her back on me and walked out of the room. She was going to have some kind of reaction to my real identity, and I'd have to deal with whatever excitement that knowledge caused. Whether I had the energy to deal with that kind of silliness was another thing altogether.

I waited. Maybe the truth of my identity hadn't really sunk in yet. The screaming and hysterical laughter would probably start any minute now.

Any minute.

I heard nothing but some muffled banging from somewhere else in the house. No screams. No laughter. No fangirl bouncing up and down and begging me for an autograph.

I sighed.

This was good, actually, because I hated fangirl bouncing and screaming. Jeremy had loved it, eaten it up. But Jeremy had been an extrovert and I was not. At all. Being pawed by fans wasn't my idea of fun.

Still, I sat on the bed and waited a few more minutes for a delayed reaction from Nova. I couldn't think of a time when I'd met a woman close to my own age—or even an older one—who hadn't gotten all flustered and silly when she recognized me. But I was starting to wonder if Nova might be an exception.

Maybe she didn't like my work. Maybe she was one of those people who automatically disliked anything popular. I didn't know whether to hate her or admire her for it.

She didn't come back.

The banging in the kitchen continued. I got out of bed, walking on unsteady legs across a plank floor to the closet where she claimed there were clothes. Inside were a few measly stacks of ancient T-shirts and sweats. The ones on the top had a layer of dust. Not up to my usual standards, but hell, I needed clothes. Nova probably wouldn't appreciate it if I walked around bare-assed naked. The feeling was not mutual, though. I'd love to see her with nothing on.

I had to sit on the edge of the bed to get dressed because my head was still woozy and everything hurt like hell. I pulled the T-shirt over my head, trying not to think about her story of finding me in the river. Because that was fucked up. Shouldn't I remember something like that? But there was nothing, just a blank space where my memories should be. I wasn't even sure why I was no longer in L.A.

Rooting around in the blankness of my mind just made my headache about ten times worse without turning up any kind of explanation as to how and why I'd gotten myself lost somewhere in Oregon. The last thing I could remember was meeting with Cindy, my personal assistant. She'd had a script someone wanted me to read.

Jesus. Would the memories ever come back? Or would I be stuck with a hole in my mind? At least I knew my name.

Wait...

I opened my wallet and took a look at my driver's license just to make sure I hadn't imagined the whole famous actor thing. No, there I was. The address even looked familiar.

So I knew who I was, just not how I'd gotten here. Or where here was.

I hobbled out of the room into a completely unfamiliar hallway. It was narrow, paneled with roughly planed wood of some kind. Not pine, because it didn't have any big, ugly knots. That was all I knew about wood.

There were pictures on the wall, mostly nature drawings. They all looked like they'd been made by the same artist.

After just twelve feet or so, the hall opened into a small kitchen on one side and a living room on the other. Nova was in the kitchen, standing at a stove that looked like it had come through a time warp from the nineteenth century. It stood on fancy metal legs and had a powdery-looking black surface and no regular controls that I could see.

She was cooking scrambled eggs and had some kind of wire thing with slices of bread in it sitting on the stove top. She glanced up at me with a smile that made my heart pound faster.

She wore no make-up. Her thick, dark hair was drawn back in a ponytail. She had on black yoga pants and a gray fleece tunic that covered her butt and upper thighs. I could see the curve of her ass through the clingy fabric of the tunic, and it was a very fine ass.

"Are you up to eating?" she said.

"Yeah. Sure."

She pulled a couple of plates out of a cupboard and plated the food. "Sit down."

"You don't have to wait on me."

"I know. But I want to make sure you're okay."

A fragment of memory came back to me, something about her pestering me to drink hot tea. "Do you take care of a lot of people?" I took a chair at the shabby wooden table in the corner.

"Not really." She set a plate in front of me. "But you had me worried. I couldn't call for help. My phone got ruined when I pulled you out of the water and the land lines are down because of the storm."

"Where are we, anyway?" I glanced out the window. Thick snow fell relentlessly, blotting out the view. All I could see was white.

"We're in Subalpine, a little town in the Cascades. There's not much here except for a few ski chalets, and it isn't really ski season yet so it's pretty deserted."

I stuck my fork into a clump of eggs. "I've never even heard of it."

"You don't remember falling in?" she said, taking the chair opposite me.

I glanced at her, wondering if she'd be open to a little hook-up action before I left. She didn't look like the type, but I'd never had any trouble getting women to fall in bed with me. And I wanted this one, wanted her with an intensity that surprised me.

"Gage?" she said gently.

"Huh? Oh, yeah. I mean, no. I don't remember it at all."

"Nothing?"

"Nope. Just ... you tried to get me to drink tea or something."

She smiled, but she looked disappointed. "Yeah, I did. You didn't want to cooperate."

I gave her my panty-dropping wink. "I didn't give you any trouble, did I?"

The blush that came over her cheeks was adorable. "No. Well, yeah, you did, but it was okay."

Reaching across the table, I laid my hand over hers. She felt delicate under my paw. How had someone so slender managed to pull me out of a river?

"Thank you, Nova," I said, making my voice soft, with maybe a hint of seduction. "I mean it. You saved my life."

"You're welcome." Damn, she looked sincere. "I was glad to do it."

"And you really didn't know who I was?"

Her eyes clouded and she pulled her hand away. "No. I'm sorry. I don't mean to offend you, but I'm not really current on pop culture."

"I'm not offended," I said casually, trying to cover the sting of her not recognizing me.

What the hell was wrong with me, anyway? I hated being recognized everywhere I went. Hated having girls and women—of all ages imaginable—throwing themselves at me like I was some kind of prize they could show off to their friends. Men, too, sometimes.

The man called Gage Dalton, the famous actor who lived his life in the public eye, was little more than a commodity. I walked through my days feeling like a fraud, a fake, someone who hadn't earned his fame and who was merely playing a part even in his so-called private life. I didn't even know who I was inside, who I was when I wasn't playing the role of Gage Dalton, famous actor.

I didn't want to be hollow anymore but it was all I knew. How did I go about being real?

It suddenly dawned on me that I'd been partying all these months since Jeremy died as a way of avoiding answering that question. Because maybe there was no answer. Maybe the famous-actor mask was all of me.

Funny. For years, I'd privately wished I could go somewhere no-one would recognize me, where I didn't have to watch everything I said and did. And now that I had a woman who didn't know—didn't even seem to care—who I was, I resented it.

"I don't watch much TV or go to many movies," she said.

That was unusual. "How come?"

"I'm a pre-med student. I'm always studying." She sneaked a bashful glance at me. "I've heard of you, of course. I just didn't recognize you. I haven't seen any of your movies."

"That's okay," I said, feeling magnanimous. "Not everyone likes the kind of thing I do."

"Oh, no, it's not that. I'm just really busy, like I said." She played with her fork, her movements sharp and nervous. "Until I moved here, I didn't do much besides study. I'm really kind of boring."

"I don't think so."

She flushed again. "It's nice of you to say that."

She was an innocent, that was obvious. I couldn't even imagine her at the kind of parties I went to, mingling with the snarky, bitchy women I'd dated. At the moment, I couldn't imagine myself with them either.

On closer inspection, Nova was clearly not the kind of girl for a casual hook-up, and after Jer's death that was the only kind of relationship I could have with her. I didn't want to risk a woman getting close to me, only to have *him* come after her. And if I couldn't hook up with her, there was no point in sticking around longer than necessary.

"I hate to put you to even more trouble," I said, "but since I don't have a car, I'd really appreciate if you could drive me into town. Then I'll be out of your hair, which I'm sure will be a relief."

"I'd like to help you there, but I can't."

I frowned, noting that she hadn't denied wanting me out of her hair. "Why not?"

"Look at the weather." She gestured toward the window. "It's crazy out there. Not safe at all. We could end up in a ditch or worse, and with you still not completely well ... I think it's a bad idea."

"You could loan me your car. I'll pay you for it."

"No." She met my gaze head-on. "I'm sorry, but I can't let you do that."

I scowled as irritation began to rise in my chest. "Can't or won't?"

"Whatever. I'm not letting you or anyone else drive my truck in that storm. Especially not you."

She knew who I was, had to know I was good for the price of the car, and she still wouldn't cooperate. Had she heard about my DUI? There had only been one, and I'd been extra careful since then.

"You don't trust me," I said, unable to keep my annoyance out of my voice.

"It's not that. Like I said, it's not safe. I didn't pull you out of the river so you could go and kill yourself on the road."

I rolled my eyes. "I know how to drive, Nova."

"No, you don't." She rolled her eyes right back at me. "You're from California and you've probably never seen a snowflake in your life."

Her smart-ass answer made me laugh a little in spite of myself. "You really won't let me borrow your car?"

"Nope."

"Great." I looked out the window again. It was a crazy storm. "So I'm stuck here."

Chapter 11
Stuck

Nova:

I glanced around the humble kitchen with its wooden counters, archaic wood-burning cookstove, handmade curtains. Some people liked rustic. Others expected everything to be slick, smoothed out, glamorous.

He made it sound so awful, being stuck in the cabin with me. Like I was his worst nightmare as a companion ... and I probably was. I sure had no glamour at all and was probably one of the least trendy women he'd ever met. I mean, look at me. No make-up, hair scraped back in a ponytail, dressed in beat-up old yoga pants and a fleece top that added at least ten visual pounds to my frame. Why would he want to hang around with me?

Although a few minutes earlier, I could have sworn he was flirting with me...

It didn't matter if he was. No amount of flirting, or money either, would make me turn my car over to him. If he died because I caved in to his pressure, I'd blame myself. Besides, I didn't want him to die, even if he was kind of spoiled and obnoxious at times.

He was here, in my cabin, and he'd been injured. He needed my care. So no matter how irritating he was, no matter how embarrassing my attraction to him, I had to put up with it until he could safely leave.

Feeling confused and resentful, I gathered the breakfast dishes and brought them to the sink for washing. The cabin had no dishwasher.

"I guess my phone is shot, too," Gage said.

"I'm sure."

"Do you have a computer I can use?"

"The Internet connection here is really iffy," I said, "but you're welcome to try. I have a satellite connection, but when it snows like this, the snow blocks the signal."

He raised his eyebrows. "So no TV and no Internet?"

"Pretty much."

"What do you do for fun around here? In fact, why are you living so far from everything?"

I shrugged. "I needed to get away for a while. It's kind of a retreat."

"And you just sit around in here all day long by yourself?"

I didn't like his tone and I shot him a glare. "No. I hike and work on a personal project of mine." He didn't need to know the project was the artwork I'd neglected for years while I put everything I had into my school studies.

"Huh." He sounded completely confounded by my explanation.

"I guess you're just going to have to put up with my boring company."

When I realized the childishness of my remark, I wanted to hide my face. I wasn't usually so snippy. This guy brought something out in me that I didn't like.

"I've got to bring some firewood in," I said, and left the kitchen.

He followed me to the back door. "Let me help."

"No. You need to stay inside where it's warm." I didn't look at him as I crammed my feet into high winter boots.

"You shouldn't have to do all this work for me on your own."

"I'm used to it." I stuffed my arms into my coat sleeves. "And it isn't just for you. I need the heat, too. Go sit down, Gage. There are some books in the living room if you feel like reading."

He glared at me for a minute. "Fine. But I'm only agreeing because you don't have a coat that would fit me."

"Or boots."

"Yeah, that too."

"I'll be back in a minute." I opened the door and walked out into the snow.

Everything looked more beautiful when the snow fell thick like this. It put a white glaze on the world, like frosting, covering over imperfections and making everything look soft. I loved the sound it made, too, the almost silent shushing of millions of snowflakes hitting the ground. The river, usually so loud, was muffled by the snowfall.

I scrunched my way to the woodpile and selected an armful. The snow was inconvenient, but the quiet of it made my irritation at Gage fade a little. He was only temporary, anyhow. Soon he'd be gone and my life would go back to its normal routine. I just had to hold onto my sanity until he left.

I had to admit to myself that he made me nervous. Partly because he was just so damn gorgeous. Men like that never paid me any attention at all, and having him around muddled my head. Then there was the fame thing. I'd never spent any time with a famous person before. Hell, I'd never even met a famous person before. He made me so self-conscious that I couldn't behave normally.

I needed to get over that. He was going to be with me for a few days at least, judging by the intensity of the snowfall.

Chapter 12
Wretched

Stamping the snow off my boots, I maneuvered through the door with my armload of firewood. Gage was still in the kitchen, still sitting at the table, hunched over the top. His face looked kind of pinched, like he was fighting back pain. That was bad. He shouldn't be feeling even worse than before unless something was very wrong.

I dropped the wood in the caddy next to the stove and turned to him. "What's going on? You don't look so good," I said.

He winced. "My stomach hurts. But I'll be fine. I'm sure it's just..." His wince turned to a grimace of pain. "Where's the bathroom?"

"Down the hall. Just across from the bedroom where you slept."

He shot out of his chair and staggered toward the bathroom. A minute later I heard him retching violently. The cabin was so small, it was impossible to hide sounds like that from other occupants.

He didn't come out. I found him kneeling in front of the toilet, looking utterly miserable. His hair stuck to his forehead in greasy strands, like it had been a while since he'd washed it and the oil hadn't come out even after his bath in the river.

"I don't think that's from the hypothermia," I said.

He nodded slowly. "I was feeling kind of sick when I left the party."

"Party?"

Gage looked up at me with bleary eyes. "Yeah. I just remembered. I was on my way back from a house party in Sunriver when I—" He broke off to heave into the toilet again.

I turned away, my own stomach turning.

"Jesus," he muttered. "Sorry about that."

"Don't apologize," I said with a glance over my shoulder. "It's not your fault."

"Yeah, well ... you might want to leave. I don't think I'm done yet."

"Are you sure?"

"Yeah." His voice sounded rough from the vomiting. "I don't really like people seeing me like this."

"Oh. Right. I'll be in the kitchen if you need me."

I felt kind of guilty leaving him alone, but it was understandable that he didn't want me to watch him being sick. Even regular people like me didn't enjoy being watched at moments like this, and he was a

Hollywood star. Constantly monitoring his image. With regret, I went back to the kitchen.

He was kind of an arrogant jerk, but I hated to see—or hear—him throwing up. Puking is one of my least favorite activities and it always makes me feel bad when other people are sick like that. Sympathy pains, I guess.

I washed the breakfast dishes and put them away. Gage came back into the kitchen just as I set the last plate back in the cupboard. His face looked just as pale as it had the afternoon before, except without the blue lips. He'd been looking better for a little while, and now he seemed to have regressed.

"I'm gonna hang out on your couch," he said, before turning on his bare heel and taking himself into the living room.

Apparently he wanted to spend as little time with me as possible. Well, too bad. By virtue of floating up on my part of the river bank, he was now my patient and he was going to have to put up with me.

I followed him. He shook his head at me as I walked over to the couch.

"You don't have to keep me company," he said.

"I want to know if you have a fever."

I hesitated an instant before laying my palm against his forehead. He was hot. My hand trembled as I touched him.

I had this bizarre sense of not-quite-being-there, like I was somehow outside my body observing what was happening. I think it was because he was *Gage Dalton*, for crying out loud. And I was touching his forehead, just like he was a regular person.

"I'm just a regular guy," he said softly, as if he'd read my mind. Those beautiful, blue eyes gazed up at me. "You don't need to be nervous."

I laughed—nervously. "I'm not."

"I wish I hadn't told you who I am."

"Why not?" I pulled my hand away.

"Because you were treating me like a normal person until you found out."

"I'm sorry. I don't mean to be such an idiot."

"Hey." He grabbed my hand. "I didn't mean it that way. It just gets old, you know? Having people get weird around me."

"Oh. Yeah, I can imagine." I cleared my throat. "So, I'm pretty sure you have a fever. And I think you might have picked up a virus somewhere. Or maybe there was something in the water, although the McKenzie is pretty clean so that's probably not it." Okay, now I was babbling. Not attractive.

Gage leaned his head back against the arm of the couch and closed his eyes. "I feel like shit."

"Does your stomach still hurt?"

"Yeah. I'm probably going to puke some more."

"Jeez. I'm so sorry."

He opened his eyes to a slit and peered up at me through his lashes. "Not your fault."

"I know. I just hate to see someone go through this, because I know how much the stomach flu sucks."

"What, this? I'm having a great time."

I chuckled. "I should get you something to drink."

"God, no. I'd just hurl again."

"But you need liquid. You don't want to get dehydrated."

He peered at me again, this time with a frown. "Nova, I appreciate your concern, but I really just want to be left alone."

I took a step back and stuffed my hands in my pockets. "Okay. I'll leave you alone, then."

Stupid to pout over it. Stupid to let him hurt my feelings. He was sick, and sick people tend to be cranky, plus he didn't even know me. Why would he want me hovering over him? I know I wouldn't like it if a stranger was hanging around watching me puke and do other embarrassing stuff.

Was he going to do other embarrassing stuff?

I could see we were in for some long days. He'd already tested my patience and we'd only gotten started. I wandered toward the kitchen, determined to ignore him as long as possible.

"Hey, Nova?" Gage called from the hallway.

I poked my head into the hall. "Yeah?"

How could anyone look so good while being so sick at the same time? Even greasy hair and the bags under his eyes couldn't make him look plain. The universe had given him a major advantage over all other men.

He stood in front of the door to the master bedroom, staring at me, his wallet in his hands. "Where'd my money go?"

"Your money?" I said blankly.

"Yeah. I had five hundred bucks in here and it's all gone." His tone sounded just a little accusing for my taste.

"I have no idea. I didn't even look at your wallet until this morning, when you gave it to me."

He glowered suspiciously at me. "Are you sure?"

"Yes, I'm sure."

"You know, if you took it, I'll understand. I won't be mad or anything as long as you give it back."

My jaw fell open. "If I took it? You think I stole from you?"

He looked uncertain. "If it wasn't you, then who was it? You're the only person I've seen since I left that party."

"Gee, I don't know. Maybe someone at the party stole your money. It wasn't me."

"Look, I'm not trying to be an asshole here, but this seems kinda suspicious."

I glowered back at him. "Yeah? I dragged you out of the river. I saved your life. Why the hell would I steal from you?"

He just continued to stare at me, his gaze boring into me like he wanted to turn me inside out. Maybe he thought I was hiding his money in a body cavity. That thought made me want to laugh, which probably would have pissed him off even more so I bit down hard on my lip.

He opened the wallet and poked through it. "Some of my credit cards are missing, too."

"Gage, I swear to you I didn't take them. But if you don't believe me, you're welcome to search the cabin." All he'd find was the twenty dollars in cash I currently had in my purse. I didn't carry wads of cash around like some big spender.

He considered my offer for another minute, staring at me the whole time. Then he pressed his hand to his belly. He disappeared into the bathroom, and an instant later I heard more retching. He was in a bad way.

He didn't know me, so part of me couldn't blame him for suspecting me. Five hundred dollars would be a major temptation to a lot of people. But another part of me thought I should boot him out into the storm for being such an ungrateful jerk.

I don't want to be an asshole.

Didn't he know there was an easy solution to that? You don't want to be an asshole ... then don't be an asshole. There were a dozen ways he could have approached me about the money loss without accusing me of being the thief.

I filled my teakettle with water and set it on the stove top. I'd gotten very little sleep, and that always made me testy and irritable. Maybe I could stay away from him until we both felt better, and then we'd be able to get along and not bite each other's heads off.

More sounds of vomiting came from the bathroom. He was going to end up dehydrated if he didn't replace some of the liquid he was tossing into the toilet. Dehydration was dangerous, and the worse it got the more nauseated he would get and the more resistant he'd be to taking liquid. It could become a vicious, even deadly, cycle.

I didn't want to argue with him again about drinking something, but I wanted a dying man on my hands even less.

My feet lagged as I walked down the short hallway to the bathroom. Confronting this guy was not high on my list of fun times. But I had a responsibility to take care of him since he was my guest. Plus, I hadn't dragged him from the river just so he could die from puking his guts out in my bathroom.

He sat on the floor, his back against the wall opposite from the toilet. His eyes were closed when I paused in the doorway. He looked awful. Beautiful, yet awful—his hair even more lank and greasy, the circles beneath his eyes a purple-black shade like two bruises, his forehead damp with sweat.

He opened his eyes and stared at me. "What do you want?" he said, his voice flat but raspy.

"You need to drink something."

"No way."

"You're going to get dehydrated."

His lids closed again. "Nova, I already told you no. It would only make me puke more."

"If you drink it super slowly, it might stay down. I'm serious, Gage. You could die out here. There's no way to call for help, and besides there aren't any real medical facilities around here. I have to take care of you, even if you don't want me to."

"Fuck," he muttered. His hand came up to push some hair from his eyes. He was trembling.

That scared me. He was vulnerable after his accident in the McKenzie, and whatever bug he had might make him a lot sicker than he would have been if he hadn't fallen into the water.

I turned silently away and went to the kitchen for a glass of cold water. When I came back, Gage was still in the same position, his head against the wall, his eyes closed. He didn't look like he was relaxed, though. It was more like he was catching his breath until the next attack of vomiting hit him.

"Here," I said, bending down with the glass.

His eyes opened. He frowned. "Damn it, I told you no."

"You're going to drink this." I held out the glass.

"No, I'm not."

"Yes, you are."

Jeez, we sounded like a couple of third-graders.

"Take that away before I throw up all over you."

"No." I thrust the glass into his hand and closed his fingers around it. "Drink extra slowly, super-tiny sips. Like you're only wetting your tongue."

His lips tightened as he glared at me. "You're damn pushy, you know that?"

"Just drink it." He could call me names all he wanted, but I still wasn't letting him die on me.

"Jesus." He lifted the glass to his lips and tilted it. "Happy now?"

"I'll be happy when"—*you're gone*—"you've finished the whole glass."

His nostrils flared. Boy, he was intimidating when he looked at me like that. But it wasn't going to work. I didn't care if he liked me or hated me. He was going to stay hydrated, even if he despised me for it.

"Would you like to go to the bedroom to drink that, or do you want to stay on the bathroom floor?" I asked sweetly.

He scowled at me for another minute before answering. "Bedroom."

I took the glass from him and watched him climb to his feet. He looked pretty unsteady, but I didn't offer to help him walk. Maybe it was petty of me. Maybe I should have been nicer. Honestly, he was starting to piss me off with his attitude.

Once we'd made it to the bedroom, he sat on the edge of the bed, his movements stiff, and took the glass from me. I folded my arms over my chest as I waited for him to take another sip. Which he did, still scowling resentfully at me.

"You're going to keep after me until I drink this whole thing, aren't you?" he said.

"Yep."

He shook his head, then winced. "My head is killing me."

"Dehydration can cause a headache."

"What are you, a doctor?"

"No," I said. "But my parents are."

He gave a short laugh. "I can believe it."

"The thing is," I continued, "dehydration makes you nauseated. And you're already nauseated, but the dehydration will only make it worse until you truly can't keep anything down. So we've got to head it off now, before it gets too much for us to handle. If it gets that bad, the only thing that will help you is an IV drip, which I don't have on hand."

He groaned. "Okay, fine, Dr. Nova. I'll try to follow orders."

"You have no idea how happy that makes me."

One corner of his mouth curled up in a half-hearted smile. "I'm sure it thrills you."

"Take another sip."

It surprised me when he followed my order. I'd half expected him to refuse again, even though he'd just promised me he would drink it.

"So, is this your place?" he said as he lowered the glass.

"It belongs to my parents."

"I'm surprised they'd let you stay out here by yourself."

"They know I'm competent."

He lifted the glass again in a mock toast. "Yes, you are."

If he was trying to be nice, it wasn't working. He just sounded like a condescending jerk. But I stayed where I was, answering questions about the area, until he'd finally gotten the whole glass of water down.

"We'll see if you can keep it down before I give you another one," I said.

"Yes, ma'am." He leaned gingerly back on the pillows and closed his eyes.

"Do you want to be alone?"

Now, why had I asked him that? I should have simply left. If he really wanted me, he could ask for my company.

"Never mind," I muttered as I left the room.

Chapter 13
November Daye

Gage:

I kept my eyes closed and listened to her soft footsteps as she left the room. The bed felt soft under my body and the air held the evocative smell of woodsmoke, but I could still taste the sourness of puke in my mouth. Even a glass of water hadn't gotten rid of all of it.

She hated me. You'd think I wouldn't give a shit, considering how bad I felt, but it bothered me. As crappy as my body felt, my mind was drawn to her, even though I couldn't explain why.

She was bossy, snippy, and just plain irritating. Did she really think I was going to die on her just because I was throwing up? And would it kill her to show a little sympathy?

She acted like I was this terrible burden on her. It's not like I expected her to hold my hand while I puked. I didn't think I was getting in her way. Not too much, anyway.

Okay, so maybe having a puking stranger in your extra bedroom wasn't especially pleasant. Maybe I was getting in her way. And maybe I was cramping her style, keeping her from all those killer parties she'd be at if it weren't for me. Oh, wait. All she did was hang around this cabin and work on her mysterious project, so probably not.

The truth was, I'd never met a girl who didn't try to throw herself at me. Except for a handful of lesbians, maybe. All the straight girls were all over me, all the time. But Nova hardly even looked at me.

I was one shallow bastard. Didn't know what to do with a woman who wasn't begging me to do her.

The last round of puking had settled my stomach a little, but it was starting to hurt again. I breathed slowly and deeply through my nose to try to settle it down. The cabin smelled like woodsmoke, and aside from some muffled noises from the kitchen was utterly silent.

This kind of quiet was foreign to me. I'd grown up in L.A., where there was no such thing as quiet, especially in the low-life neighborhoods where my mom and I had lived until I started making money. There was always some kind of man-made noise in my hometown.

Traffic noise, sirens, garbage trucks, car stereos, planes overhead, neighbors hollering at each other, a constant dull roar twenty-four hours a day.

Here there was nothing except the wind in the trees, and right now I couldn't even hear that. When I glanced out the window, all I saw was a constantly falling curtain of white.

I started to shiver. I wasn't sure if the cabin was really cold or if it was just me. Either way, I wrapped the blankets around me and tried to get warm. My efforts didn't seem to be working.

A few minutes later, my gut cramped violently. I threw off the blankets and staggered to the bathroom, reaching it just in time. Jesus. What a thing to have when there was a beautiful stranger right in the next room. I cringed, hoping she couldn't hear me.

Not long after I crawled back into bed, she came into my room. "How do you feel?" she said softly.

"Like crap."

"Did you throw up the water?"

"No." I closed my eyes, half hoping she'd go away and half hoping she'd stay. Maybe crawl into bed with me.

She came over to me, her feet making soft noises on the old throw rug that covered the simple wooden floor. Her little hand pressed gently against my forehead. She smelled good, like smoke and vanilla.

"You're still hot," she said.

So are you.

"Will I live, doc?" My voice sounded almost unrecognizable.

"Your prognosis is good." She had a smile in her voice. Maybe I was getting to her. Finally.

Did I want to get to her? I'd already decided she wasn't the usual party girl type I took to bed. She seemed like the type to get emotionally involved, and I couldn't do that to her. I couldn't drag her into the dark ugliness of my life, expose her to the same shit that had killed Jeremy.

Normally, I wouldn't be so ethical. I mean, I didn't even like her. Not really. I just found her weirdly fascinating and sexually attractive. So why hold back? We could have a good time for a while, after I'd gotten better. Then I'd go on my way and we'd both be happy.

But what if something bad happened to her because of me? What if *he* really was following me around and picking off anyone I got close to? I couldn't repay her generosity by endangering her.

No, Dr. Nova was not for me.

"I wish I had something for you to do to pass the time," she said.

"I'm fine."

The light flickered and went out, leaving only the chill gray light coming through the window.

"Well, there goes the electricity." She sounded way too cheerful about it.

"Does this happen a lot?"

"I think so. This is the first winter I've spent up here, but from what I hear from the locals, it's pretty common."

I grunted in acknowledgment. Having the electricity go out would suck. Or would it? On further thought I realized I didn't much care about it. I felt too shitty to want to do anything but lay here anyway. She had that wood-burning cook stove, so we wouldn't be cold.

"I could read to you."

I pried my eyes open and found her smiling at me. "Are you serious?"

"Not really. But I would if you wanted me to."

"Uh ... no, thanks." Most people had no idea how to read something aloud and make it sound interesting, and that made their awkward performances painful to endure.

"Okay. Well, if you need anything, just holler." She got up.

I did need something. I needed her lips on mine. She wouldn't want to give me that, and I couldn't think of anything else that would make me feel as good, so I kept my mouth shut.

"Do you think you could get another glass of water down?" she said, pausing in the doorway.

"Maybe."

"Then I'll be right back."

She was persistent for sure. I couldn't blame her for not wanting a dead body on her hands, and I didn't want to die anyway, so I'd cooperate. For now.

If I let myself die, my mom would probably be relieved. She'd know the devil wasn't coming after her, since he'd already gotten what he wanted. Maybe I should just let myself go. Let's face it—the world didn't need me. All I did was entertain people, just another pretty face on the big screen. Who would miss me?

And maybe it really should have been me instead of Jeremy. I'd always thought he'd turned to drugs because of some of the crazy shit that went down in our world, shit that had bypassed me because of The Deal. I'd had an unfair advantage.

Problem was, I wasn't ready. I didn't want to go, even if I'd be doing everyone else a favor if I did.

Nova reappeared carrying another glass of water. I couldn't do it to her, even if I had the power to let myself die. She didn't deserve to be stuck with my corpse.

Grudgingly, I levered myself into a sitting position. She sat on the edge of the bed next to me and handed me the glass with a shy smile. A smile! I felt like I'd won a prize.

I smiled back at her. "Listen, I'm sorry I've been so grouchy. I'm not usually like this."

She waved a hand negligently. "Don't worry about it."

"I've been really rude to you and you don't deserve that. I'm grateful to you for getting me out of the river and everything."

She gave me a sidelong glance full of meaning that I couldn't decipher. "Okay. I appreciate you telling me that."

I took one of her tiny sips of water. "I'm really lucky you came along when you did, huh?"

"Yeah, you are. I don't think you would have lived much longer in the river."

An uncomfortable silence settled over us. I watched her as I drank a little more water. Her thick, dark hair hung halfway down her back in a ponytail. Just like the day before, she had no make-up and her nails were plain. She hadn't gone to any trouble over me, hadn't tried to make herself look more glamorous because I was here. Her manner had changed, too. She didn't seem so nervous anymore.

Bossing me around must have made her feel a whole lot better. I fought back a smirk as I considered the possibilities of her continuing to boss me around, maybe while naked ... but, no. I'd already decided to leave her alone.

"I've never met anyone named Nova before," I said. "Were you named after the car?"

"No." She laughed. "It's short for November."

"November. Never met anyone named that, either."

"My birthday is this month and I guess my mom was feeling creative when she named me," she said, blushing a little. She was cute when she blushed. The color stained her high cheekbones and almost climbed the bridge of her straight little nose.

"What's your full name?" I said.

She glanced at me again, looking slightly embarrassed. "November Daye Pennyman."

"November Daye." I grinned. "That's different."

"Yes, it is." She paused, plucking nervously at the comforter. "I've never met anyone named Gage either."

"It's not my real name." Shit. Why had I said that? I never told anyone about the name change. Even Jer hadn't known.

"It's not?" Her brows raised. "What is your real name, then?"

"Robert." I shrugged. "My mom claims that was my dad's choice, although I've always wondered because he didn't stick around very long. When I got into show business, she decided a trendier name would be better for my image."

Okay. My mouth seemed to have its own agenda today.

"Oh." Nova blinked those long-lashed, honey-colored eyes. "How old were you?"

"Ten." I'd told my mom I just wanted to be plain old Rob, but she didn't care and I was too young at the time to really assert myself.

Nova tilted her head, studying me. "Which one do you like better?"

"I've been Gage so long it feels like my real name."

"So that's what you want me to call you?"

"Yeah, sure." Did it really matter? I'd only be here a few days at the most.

Chapter 14

Stay

Nova:

The master bedroom, not especially big in the first place, felt way too small after that last exchange with Gage. I couldn't stay here with him, not right now.

He'd gotten the strangest look on his face right after he'd told me his real name. Like he wished he could take the words back. He regretted telling me.

I walked away from him, wishing I could quit getting my feelings hurt over this stuff. What did I care if he did or didn't want to tell me his real name? It's not like we were in a relationship.

Oh, Nova. Don't even go there.

Shit. Was I harboring some fluffy-headed wish that he'd fall for me? That he'd look at me and see a desirable woman instead of a frumpy recluse? That the fact I'd saved his life would somehow translate into love?

I winced. Inwardly, where no-one could see me.

And then came the lecture.

Listen up, self. 1: life is not a romance novel. Hot movie stars don't fall in love with boring nobodies they meet in the sticks. 2: you couldn't even hold on to Barry. What makes you think a god like Gage Dalton would be interested in doing anything with you other than talking?

And he didn't seem especially interested in talking, come to think of it.

I'd been up here on the mountain by myself too long. That was my problem. I was lonely. Yeah, there were other folks around here, but I didn't see them too often. It was probably time to quit this self-imposed exile and get back to my real life.

A twinge of dread curled in my belly at the thought of going back to non-stop studying and I realized I had no plan for my life after the cabin. I'd spent all my time up here drawing and painting instead of thinking about my future.

If I went back now, nothing would have changed except I'd be without a boyfriend and a best friend. Was that what I wanted?

I made myself some tea and sat down at the kitchen table to drink it. The stove made this room warm, which was a pleasant change from the chilly master bedroom. I thought of Gage all alone in that room and didn't know whether to feel sorry for him or annoyed.

He'd told me to leave, so it's not like I'd abandoned him. My job right now was to care for him while staying distant and unattached. Hovering over him all the time would not accomplish my goal.

I got out my sketchbook and started making some abstract designs to pass the time. I wasn't feeling it today. Having a sick movie star in my cabin was distracting ... go figure.

I kinda got lost in my drawing anyway, and when I looked up the battery-powered clock hanging on the wall told me two hours had passed. What was Gage doing? He hadn't made a sound since I'd come out here.

He didn't want me hovering. But on the other hand, I needed to make sure he was okay. What if he'd gotten worse while I sat here making art?

Sighing, I left my art on the table and went back to the bedroom. I peeked inside, hoping to catch him naked. No, no, that's not what I hoped. Not at all. I ... hoped he was all right and not naked, because I didn't want either of us to get embarrassed again.

Really. That's what I wanted.

He was curled on his side, almost in a fetal position, the old, blue, hand-tied quilt my mom had made some time back in the early nineties pulled up part way over his head. He was shivering. I could see the comforter twitching as he moved underneath it.

And I know how it might seem, but it wasn't that. He wasn't having a moment of intimacy with himself; he was really sick.

His eyes were closed, making me think he was asleep. I crept closer, hoping I wouldn't wake him. I just wanted to get close enough to touch him, to make sure he wasn't as sick as he looked.

I leaned over him. His breath stuttered in and out, as if he couldn't even work his lungs smoothly. I laid my hand on his forehead, wishing I had a thermometer. Stupid oversight, especially for a doctor's daughter.

He still felt hot, but not dangerously hot. He probably just had chills, the kind you often get when you've got a nasty virus.

One blue eye opened. "Hey," he rasped.

"Hi. You don't look so good."

"Feel like shit."

I frowned. "Do you have a dry mouth?" His lips looked normal, pink and slightly moist. Kissable.

Damn it. I was doing it again.

"No dry mouth," he said.

Probably not dangerously dehydrated, then. "The virus is probably just giving you chills. I'll let you get some sleep." I started to move away, when a heavy male arm snaked around my waist. My heart started pounding heavily.

"Stay," he said.

I paused. "Are you sure?"

"Yeah. I'd like you to stay."

He hadn't used the magic word. Maybe he didn't know it? I'd bet he didn't have much use for it in his everyday life. People probably turned themselves into pretzels trying to please him and give him everything he wanted. I was not going to be one of those people.

But he looked so vulnerable beneath that comforter, so alone. Almost ... sad.

Nah. I was just imagining things.

"You don't have to if you don't want to," he whispered. "I just—"

"Okay." I sat on the bed next to him. God, I was easy.

His arm remained around my waist and I didn't have the heart to tell him to remove it. Okay, that's not really true. I just liked it there, liked the way he felt against me. My ass was snugged up next to his rib cage and the position gave me the illusion we were something more than we really were.

I wanted to savor that illusion for a few minutes, knowing it would be over way too soon.

He kept shivering. Sometimes his teeth rattled together the way they had right after I'd pulled him from the water. His eyes stayed closed, and he didn't talk. He just lay there holding me around the waist and looking miserable.

I wanted to comfort him, make his pain go away. It was probably just my fantasies telling me this, but the hurt he was feeling seemed to come from something a lot deeper than a tummy bug. I lifted my hand and hesitantly pushed the damp hair from his forehead. His hold on my waist tightened, just enough to let me know it was a response to my touch.

"I wish there was something I could do to make you feel better," I said.

"You are."

I was such an idiot. I was the queen of all romantic idiots, because when he said that, a sweet warm glow came over me. Almost like he'd said that he—you know—cared for me.

He didn't say anything after that. I sat and waited for him to fall asleep, but I couldn't tell if he was or not. Outside, the storm raged just as heavily, making me wonder if we'd have to dig our way out.

I was so tired. Exhausted. I'd been awake most of the night, worrying about Gage, and my body was still worn out from all the work I'd done the day before. My eyes didn't want to stay open.

I glanced down at him. He looked like he was sleeping. He probably wouldn't mind if I just stretched out beside him, right?

Carefully, trying not to force him to shift, I lowered myself to the mattress. He pulled me closer, spooning us. With his long, hard heat behind me, my body began to warm, the place between my thighs pulsing softly. This was so wrong. I was getting turned on—again—by him, and he wasn't even awake.

"You smell really good," he whispered.

Okay, scratch that. He was totally awake.

"Um ... thanks." I made to get up, but he wouldn't let me go.

"Please," he said. "I really like having you here."

"You do?" This didn't come out all breathy and flirtatious. It was more disbelieving.

"Yeah. Is it okay if I hold you like this?"

"Uh ... sure. I guess so."

He didn't answer right away, and I wondered if he'd finally fallen asleep. He probably needed it even more than I did.

I'd missed this kind of body contact. The only touch I'd gotten in months was some brief hugs from my family. Nothing like this. No holding, no snuggling since I'd broken up with Barry. Plus, Barry hadn't been much for snuggling anyway.

Gage wouldn't stick around. I knew that. But this experience told me I needed a lot more human contact of all kinds. I didn't belong here, hiding out by myself. When the storm was over, I'd be leaving.

I just had to decide how I was going to tell my parents I didn't want to be a doctor after all. They weren't going to like hearing that.

Chapter 15

Promise

Gage:

Her body felt more comforting than anything I'd experienced in a long time, snuggled up to mine, warm and soft. She smelled good, like smoke and vanilla. I took a cautious sniff of her hair, keeping it quiet so she wouldn't notice and think I was creeping on her.

Was I putting Nova in danger just by holding her like this? I didn't think so. It wasn't real; we weren't in a real relationship, and we hadn't made any commitments to each other. We'd only just met.

But it felt real. All I'd done was put my arm around her, yet it felt more real than anything I'd had in a long time.

Not. Real.

I was sick. I felt like shit, and I was alone in a strange place. She was beautiful and she smelled good and she'd been kind to me, even if she was too bossy. That's all this feeling was, and that's all it would ever be. Reminder to self: you cannot get involved emotionally with anyone.

In fact, I shouldn't be using her for comfort like this. I should let her get up and do whatever it was she normally did all day. Laying around with a sick dude, especially one who smelled like I did at the moment, couldn't be any woman's idea of a good time.

I'd let her go in a few minutes. I just wanted to enjoy this warmth for a little longer.

"I was pretty high at the party," I said in a low murmur.

Christ, what was wrong with me? I couldn't control my mouth around her. It must be the atmosphere in this place. We were shut in together, snow falling like crazy outside, everything quiet inside. The cabin felt remote, almost otherworldly, and I guess that encouraged me to open up to her.

Nova shifted in my arms. "You were high?"

"Yeah." I was reluctant to talk about it now, but it was too late. I'd opened my big damn mouth. "I was pretty ripped for a few days, actually."

"You do that often?"

I tried to detect some disapproval or disappointment in her voice, but I couldn't find any.

"Uh ... yeah," I said. "I used to anyway."

It occurred to me that I probably wouldn't have fallen in the water if I hadn't been both high and drunk at the time. I could have died. Sheer, dumb luck was the only thing that had saved me. That, and Nova.

I couldn't keep living this way, and when I got home I was going to do something about it. Get counseling. Something.

"Did you have drugs in your system when you fell in?" Nova said.

"Yeah, I did. Alcohol, too."

"You're lucky you survived." She twisted in my arms until she'd rolled over to face me. "Promise me you won't do that anymore."

I stared at her in astonishment. Why would she care? She didn't know me.

She blushed under my stare and her gaze fell. "I'm sorry. I had no right to say that to you."

I lifted my hand to her cheek. Her skin was so soft. "I think it's sweet that you care."

Nova gave her head a tiny shake. "I'm sure a lot of people care about you."

As a cash cow, yeah. As a person, not so much. "You'd be surprised."

Her gaze flicked up to meet mine. She had the most beautiful eyes, big and wide and golden brown, with long curled black lashes.

"I think you're wrong," she said softly. "I can't imagine people not caring about you."

Damn, that was sweet. Did she really mean it or was she just flattering me? Nova didn't seem like the type for empty flattery.

"I don't have the greatest friends," I said. It seemed like this was the day for nonstop confessions. My attempts to say distant didn't seem to be working.

No emotional involvement.

Her face fell. "Yeah, I think I know what you mean."

"Are you telling me you used to hang out with a rough crowd, Nova?" I teased.

"No. I'm as boring as they come. But the reason I came out here..." She bit her lip. "I caught my boyfriend cheating on me with my best friend."

"Shit." I had a sudden desire to strangle that asshole, and I didn't even know his name.

She laughed a little. "You could say that."

"You mean you actually caught them together?"

"Uh huh. They were—you know—doing it on the couch. In the apartment I shared with her."

"I'm really hating on your best friend right now," I said.

She smiled. "Thanks."

"Don't mention it. And your ex-boyfriend must be a dumbass, in addition to being a douchecanoe for cheating on you."

She laughed again. "Douchecanoe?"

"Definitely."

"That's funny. I don't think anyone has ever called Barry that before." She was still staring at me, smiling, her eyes all crinkled up in the corners.

"Give me his phone number and I'll text him with it," I said. "He deserves it for hurting you."

"It was so weird seeing them together. I didn't even think they liked each other."

"So you decided to hide out for a while?"

"Yeah." She frowned a little. "I thought I could figure things out. Figure out why it was so easy for him to cheat on me. Figure out what I wanted to do with my life."

"He cheated on you because he's an asshat," I said. "It wasn't you."

Her gaze fell as her lips pressed together.

"No, seriously." I cupped the side of her face with my hand. "You're great. There's no way you deserved what he did."

Those golden-brown eyes of hers stared at me like she was trying to see my thoughts. I couldn't tell if she believed me or not about her ex, but I was totally serious. Only an idiot would cheat on a girl like her, an idiot who didn't know or appreciate what he had.

"Do you promise me?" Nova said.

"Huh?" I blinked, confused at the sudden change of subject.

"You never gave me your word. Do you promise me not to abuse drugs again?"

"Um ..." I stroked her cheek with my thumb. I didn't want to lie to her, but I didn't want to disappoint her, either. This was new for me—normally, I couldn't have cared less what some girl I just met thought of my partying ways. "I can't really promise you that."

"Why not?"

God, she looked so innocent, gazing at me with those huge, brown eyes. So trusting. And what had I done to earn that trust? Nothing.

"I don't want to let you down," I said. "I don't want to make a promise I can't keep."

"But—"

I pressed my forefinger to her lips. They were as soft and warm as they looked. "I promise you I'll get help as soon as I get back to L.A."

She took a deep breath. "Okay. Good."

I smiled at her. "I don't want to end up in another freezing river. You might not be there next time to pull me out."

"That's right."

"Now you have to promise me something."

She narrowed her eyes warily. "What's that?"

"You won't go back to the douchecanoe, even if he begs."

Nova laughed. "I can't see that happening. No, I'll never go back to him."

"Good."

I let my hand descend along her arm, caressing lightly, savoring the feel of her under my touch. Her breath caught. Her eyes dilated and her lip trembled as her gaze rested on my lips. In that moment, I was sure she wanted me.

And I wanted her. God, how I wanted her. I leaned in a little, fascinated by her pretty mouth. It wouldn't be right to kiss her, though. She might get the godawful bug I had.

Then she jerked backward and tumbled off the bed. I propped myself on an elbow.

"You all right?"

"Yeah." She rose to her feet, looking abashed. "I'm fine. Um, sorry. You just kind of startled me."

Hot color stained her cheeks. I was too tired and sick to do anything sexual anyway, but her reaction to my touch deflated me pretty sharply. I must have read her wrong.

That had never happened to me before.

"I just—um—I'd better go." She motioned vaguely toward the hallway.

"Nova, I didn't mean to scare you."

"You didn't. I'm not scared. I just—you know—I've got things to do." She turned and left the room so fast it was like she was running away.

I collapsed onto my back and closed my eyes. What had just happened? I couldn't figure her out. She didn't react to me like any other woman I'd ever met and I had no idea what she'd do next.

Why did it even matter to me? I wouldn't be here very long. I'd go back to L.A. and she'd go back to wherever she'd lived before. It dawned on me that I didn't know where she was from. I didn't know anything about her, really. As I'd tried to tell myself earlier, these odd feelings I was having for her weren't real. They came out of the situation, and didn't really have much to do with her as a person.

For some reason, that knowledge didn't make me feel any less attracted to her.

I pulled the blue quilt over myself again. The vomiting seemed to have stopped, for now at least. But my gut was still churning and I didn't know when I'd need to run to the bathroom again. Until then, I'd try to get some sleep.

The instant that thought was finished, my gut spazzed out again. I threw off the covers and made for the bathroom, hoping that Nova had gone temporarily deaf.

I didn't like the general public to see—or hear—me this way. I had an image to protect, after all. I was a valuable commodity and I didn't want to damage my brand by appearing less than perfect in a public place.

This is the opposite of public. It's almost as private as things can get.

But Nova wasn't a member of my inner circle. She was an unknown quantity, an outsider, who could potentially reveal embarrassing facts about me to the media. Although she didn't seem like the kind of person who would do that, money can change people. Certain entertainment news organizations would pay a whole lot for dirt on me.

I wondered what people had made of my disappearance. I'd been gone missing long enough to cause some alarm. My mom was probably losing her mind.

If someone figured out where I was, maybe they could get me out of here. I could go back to civilization, provided they could get a vehicle up here in this storm.

I'd be out of Nova's life. We'd most likely never see each other again, unless I brought her down to Cali for a visit. I tried to picture Nova staying in my condo, all the usual hangers-on wandering in and out, and couldn't quite make it work.

No emotional attachment means no visits.

Right. No emotional attachment. I had a hunch that plan wasn't going to work out at all.

Chapter 16
Sketchbook

Nova:

I took refuge in the warmth and brightness of the kitchen. There was always something to do there—food to cook, dishes to clean—plus it was the farthest room from him. Keeping myself busy prevented me from going back in there and making a fool of myself.

Gage hobbled out of the bedroom in the middle of the afternoon. He looked pale and exhausted, but he smiled at me. My heart picked up speed at the sight of him. At the moment, all scruffy and unkempt, he didn't look like a movie star; he just looked like a good-looking guy who was feeling really bad.

He was emphatically off-limits to me. But I couldn't help my response to him; I got all fluttery every time he was near.

"Can I get a glass of water?" he said. "I'm starting to feel queasy again."

"Of course. Sit down."

I brought the glass to the table. His fingers brushed mine when I handed it to him. Although I pretended not to notice, inside I was trembling. Had he done it on purpose? When we were on the bed, I'd thought he was about to kiss me. That was why I scooted backward and fell off the bed like an idiot.

While he'd slept, I'd reminded myself over and over that Gage Dalton was not for me. Allowing myself to crush on him was stupid. It would lead me to some major mistakes if I let it, and I couldn't afford that. I had a fight on my hands just getting my parents to respect my decision about my career, and loading a teeny-bopper unrequited love on top of it would make everything ten times worse.

Unfortunately, all my sensible good intentions didn't stop me from bubbling inside with infatuation. How had he done this to me? I'd gone from disliking him to hoping he'd kiss me in less than a day.

It had to be his unmatched gorgeousness. And that voice...deep and smooth and pitched in a way I found ridiculously seductive.

Was he trying to seduce me?

I sneaked a glance at him and found him watching me. My face burned and I got a little more trembly inside.

God, how dumb. I'd watched this guy puking his guts out not so long ago. He was, in his own words, just a regular guy. Before I'd known who he was, I hadn't been overawed by him. Attracted, yeah, but not a gibbering idiot.

"So you came up here because of your boyfriend?" Gage said.

Barry was not the person I wanted to talk about. "Um...yeah. I wanted to get away, think about some things."

He glanced out the window. "It must be a good place for thinking."

"Yeah. Not much else to do around here, except fish."

"Do you fish?" he said, watching me again.

"Not much. You want some tea instead of plain water?"

"Sure." He cocked his head, still watching me. "So what's your major?"

I couldn't help it. I laughed.

"What?" He smiled.

"Nothing. That's just the most clichéd question on campus."

"Ah. Kind of like everyone asking what do you do for a living when you're at a cocktail party?"

"Exactly." I got out a couple of tea bags.

"Let me guess. Home Ec."

I had no idea why he'd picked that one. Maybe I looked like the backwoods version of Donna Reed or something. "Nope." I poured the hot water over the tea. "I'm pre-med."

"Gonna be a doctor like your parents, huh?"

"That was the plan. Do you like milk and sugar?" I asked as I got the things out for my own cup.

"Sure."

"Did you go to college?"

He paused. "No, I didn't. I've been too busy working."

"Oh." I glanced over my shoulder at him as I stirred the tea. "Do you want to go?"

He shrugged, looking uncomfortable. "Don't know what I'd study."

Had I offended him by asking that question? I hadn't meant to put him on the spot. "Well, not everyone needs a degree. I don't even know if I'll finish now."

I brought the mugs to the table and sat down across from him. His big hand closed around one of the cups and dragged it to his side. He even had beautiful fingers, long and well-shaped.

"What are you going to do if you don't become a doctor?" he said.

"I don't know. I've never given it any thought because I was always going to go to med school."

As soon as I thought it, though, my heart whispered that I could become an artist. I had no idea how to earn a living that way, or if it was even possible, but it was what spoke to me.

"I draw," I blurted. "And paint."

74

It sounded weird even saying it out loud. My parents had no idea how much time I spent these days practicing my art. I never talked about it with my family.

"An artist," Gage said. "Cool. Would you let me see your stuff?"

"Oh, I don't know." I couldn't look at him. "I'm not very good."

"So?" He reached across the table and took my hand. "I'd really like to see it sometime."

His hand felt so good around mine, and of course my silly heart started racing and fluttering and doing some kind of uncoordinated dance all at the same time. Gage was touching me. Me.

Oh, what could it hurt to show him the book? whispered my inner voice.

"I—um—my sketchbook is right there." I pointed to the windowsill.

He picked up the book. "Is it okay? You're sure?"

"Yeah, go ahead."

I waited nervously while he leafed through my drawings. He wasn't saying anything, just pausing to study each one, a serious little frown between his brows. I shouldn't have let him look. He'd probably seen all kinds of expensive, professional-level art with the lifestyle he lived and my amateurish scribblings wouldn't interest him.

"Did you do the pieces in the hallway?" he said, his voice so neutral that I had no idea what he was thinking.

"Yeah."

"You're really good, Nova."

I made a pfft sound. He was just trying to make me feel good.

"You are," he said, more emphatically. "I think you have a lot of talent. You should pursue this."

"You're serious?"

"Yeah." He gave me a perceptive glance. "Did you think I was bullshitting you?"

I shrugged, suddenly uncomfortable. "I don't know." My gaze flickered to his and then away. "I don't know what to think of you."

"I wouldn't lie to you." He touched my hand again. The brush of his skin on mine brought tingles all through my body. "I like you, and I like your work. Not everybody has this kind of talent."

"Well. Thank you." I took a sip of tea, trying to cover my confusion.

"Hasn't anyone ever told you that you're good?"

"No. I don't really show my work to most people."

"Really?" There was a smile in his voice. "Then I'm special, huh?"

"Yes, you are."

What had made me say that? He didn't need to know how I felt about him. I almost clapped my hand over my eyes. Instead, I did the less dramatic thing and closed them.

His hand tightened on mine. "I thought you disliked me."

My eyes flew open. "I don't dislike you."

"You've been kind of snappish with me." He smiled engagingly. "Not that I can blame you. I wouldn't want to be stuck with a puking stranger either."

"Oh, no. It wasn't that." Oops. I should have let it go at the puking. Now we'd have to talk about his personality.

He raised one dark eyebrow. "Then what was it?"

I was pretty sure my face was about to sprout flames. "Nothing. Never mind. I didn't mean to say that."

"Come on. Tell me."

I sneaked a look at him. He was still smiling, so maybe I hadn't pissed him off or hurt him too much. "I guess I thought you were kind of arrogant."

His smile broadened. "Oh, yeah?"

"Yeah. And difficult."

"Difficult, huh?"

Why did he think this was funny? It was killing me with embarrassment.

"Well, you did argue with me," I said in my defense. "And you wouldn't drink your water."

"I'm a terrible patient."

My lips curled up, reluctantly. "Yeah, you are."

"And I accused you of stealing from me."

I shook my head. "I can't really blame you."

"Yeah, you can. I was being a dick and I'm sorry." He squeezed my hand. "I really do apologize for that. I wasn't thinking straight."

"If you don't believe me, go ahead and search the cabin," I said. "I don't mind."

"The thing is, I wish I had that cash on me," he said. "So I could give it to you."

"What? Why would you do that?"

"For taking care of me."

"I don't expect money." I scowled at him. "I did it because it was the right thing to do, not so I could get a reward."

"Doesn't mean I can't reward you." He winked at me. "I would like to reward you, Nova."

He could make the most innocuous statements sound naughty. But he probably talked to all the girls this way; he was a born playboy and now that I thought about it, I'd heard rumors that he played the field, a different woman on his arm at every event he attended. See? Even I occasionally got hold of some Hollywood gossip.

"You don't have to do that," I said. "I'm just grateful I was there to help. I hate to think of you ... you know ..."

"Dead?"

"Yeah. That."

"Me, too." He lifted my hand to his lips and kissed me on my knuckles. "You're a sweetheart, you know that? There aren't many people like you in the world."

"Oh, come on." I scoffed to cover the giddiness that had overtaken me when his lips touched my skin. "Anyone would have done the same thing I did."

"Not true." His fingers tightened around mine. "A lot of people would have just ignored what they saw."

"No." I shook my head vigorously. "Anyone around here would have jumped in and saved you."

"Not the people I know."

Wow. I didn't know how to respond to that. What kind of friends did he have?

"Did I tell you I've been hanging around with a bad crowd?" he said lightly.

"I'm sorry."

"Don't be. It's my own fault." He began stroking the back of my hand with soft, circular movements of his thumb. "I chose my friends and I did a suck-ass job of it."

"Why is that?"

He paused, his thumb still caressing my hand. Such a seductive movement, those little circles.

"I got involved with them when I was a lot younger, when I didn't have any common sense. And then it was just ... what I knew."

"But ..." I didn't want to insult him, yet I had to ask. "If you think they're not good people, why do you keep seeing them?"

His gaze met mine, and I could see the sadness in his eyes, although I didn't know the reason for it. "That's a good question. Habit, I guess."

"Are you going to keep seeing them, now that—"

"I almost died?" he interrupted.

"Yeah."

His broad shoulders lifted carelessly. "Probably not, except when I can't avoid it."

I hardly knew anything about him, yet I had this feeling like I'd known him for years. It was just an effect of being shut up in a cabin with him for days. That and saving his life. Holding him while he was naked and unconscious. Taking care of him while he was sick. But it was a trick, an illusion of intimacy that didn't really exist. I knew this to be true, yet sitting with him like this, talking quietly, the illusion seemed more real than anything else I'd ever experienced.

"The truth is," he said softly, "I wish I had more friends like you."

Chapter 17

Faking It

Gage:

I could tell when I got up in the morning and saw her sitting at the kitchen table that Nova wasn't feeling well. It had pushed my self-control to go to bed without at least trying for a kiss from her, but I'd done it. I'd taken my horny ass to bed and tried to forget about seducing her.

She'd gotten all awkward anyway, after I'd told her I wished I had more friends like her. I should've kept my mouth shut. I could see she didn't believe me.

Now, looking at her pasty skin and the dark bags under her eyes, I knew I'd given her the stomach flu. And outside, the snow fell just as mercilessly as it had for the past two days. We wouldn't be able to get out of here and get her medical help any more than we had for me. We were still stuck together, only now I was the one who had to play nurse.

She gave me a listless smile as I came into the kitchen. She'd already started heating some water on the stove, but she was sitting down at the table, her head propped on her hand.

"Not feeling so good, huh?" I said, sitting down opposite her.

"No. I think I have what you had."

I winced in sympathy and guilt. "Sorry about that."

"It's not your fault." She pushed some limp, brown strands from her forehead. "I'm not surprised."

I didn't relish the idea of tending a woman who was going through the nastiness I'd just survived. Nursing the sick was not on my resume. But it wouldn't be right to leave her alone, even if I could have gone. And I couldn't.

Could Jeremy see me from wherever it was he'd gone? If he could, he was probably laughing his ass off at me. The so-called sexiest man alive holding a girl's hand while she puked her guts out. And I wasn't even planning on bagging her. What a joke.

Normally, I'd have bailed on her at this point. I didn't normally stay with a woman the whole night, let alone hang around to watch her get sick. But Nova was different. I would have stayed even if the roads had been clear. She'd saved my life, and even a selfish prick like me wouldn't walk away from her when she needed help.

"You're looking at me like you think I'm going to shrivel up and die," she said with a wry lift of her lips. "I'll be fine. I've been through the stomach flu before."

"So have I, but this one was different. It was a lot worse," I said.

"Yeah, but you'd fallen into a freezing river the day before. I'm healthy. I probably won't get as sick as you."

Half an hour later, she was hurling miserably into the toilet. I stayed in the hallway in an effort to avoid embarrassing her. But it sounded awful, maybe even worse than mine. She just kept heaving and heaving. Then she'd pause for a few minutes, and start heaving again.

Even I hadn't puked that many times in a row without a rest break. I wasn't much of a worrier, especially about a person I'd just met and didn't really know. But, again, Nova was different. She'd taken care of me when I needed someone ... I could admit that this morning, since I'd woken up feeling at least half-human and a lot more rational. Now it was her turn to be sick and my turn to care for someone.

I edged my way into the bathroom, a glass of water from the kitchen in my hand. "Nova. You need to drink something."

"I'm fine."

I couldn't help grinning. Our positions were reversed, and she was about to find out just how annoying it could be to have someone nag you about drinking when you felt like puking at the mere thought of food or water.

"You're throwing up at least as hard as I did," I said. "And you're the one who's so keen on staying hydrated."

She turned her head and glared at me from her crouch on the floor. She looked like hell, her skin a sickly white with purplish shadows under her eyes, her hair lank and sticking to her forehead. Weirdly, I still found her attractive.

"I'm not done yet," she said.

"You're going to start throwing up your stomach lining or something if you don't put some liquid in there," I said. I was really working this nurse thing.

In response, she turned back to the toilet and heaved into it. Nothing came out but a thin, yellowish string of bile. The sight and sound turned my stomach, too. I looked away.

"You can't help me, Gage."

I glanced at her as she wiped her mouth with the back of her hand.

"Just leave me alone," she muttered.

"Nope. Can't do that." I crouched next to her and held out the glass. "Drink something. Remember, tiny sips."

She glowered at me. I kept a serene smile on my face, holding the glass in front of her, waiting patiently for her to give in. It took a few minutes of withstanding her nasty scowl, but she finally sighed and accepted the glass.

"Tiny sips," I said.

She rolled her eyes. "Yes, Dr. Gage."

I pointed at the glass. "Drink, Miss Pennyman."

Nova tilted the glass. It was such a minuscule tilt that I couldn't tell if even a single drop had actually left the glass for her tongue.

"Are you drinking or faking it?" I said, as sternly as I could.

"I never fake it," she said. Then she blinked. Her face turned magenta.

I grinned again. "Good to know."

"I didn't mean it that way."

"Okay. Sure." I pointed again. "Drink."

She obeyed. Then she settled back against the wall, the way I had the day before, and closed her eyes. "You're having fun with this, aren't you?"

"Absolutely."

"I guess I should thank you for looking out for me." She didn't sound grateful at all. "You could go to the living room and read or something, you know. You don't have to stay with me."

"I know. But I owe you."

"No, you don't." Her voice was getting fainter.

"Drink a little more for me."

She kept her eyes closed while her brows came down. "I can't."

"Try."

"Jesus, I think I've created a monster," she muttered as she raised the glass.

"I don't want you to get dehydrated," I said piously. "We're out here in the middle of nowhere without a phone."

"Shut up, Gage." She took another invisible sip.

I laughed. Strangely, I really was enjoying being with her, even though she was sick. She never simpered over me or tried to make me want her. Sometimes that irritated the shit out of me, but it also gave me room to breathe. Room to be as normal as it was possible for me to be.

You can't really be normal when you're constantly pursued by strangers who all want a piece of you, a touch of your hand, a photo, an autograph, and sometimes more. Sometimes things you don't want to give or that you aren't capable of giving. People who claim they love you when they don't even know you. People who love their fantasies of who you are, not the real you.

I'd lived that way since I was a kid, so in a sense I was used to it. But at the same time—and I don't want to sound all self-pitying or anything, because I know I have a lot to be grateful for, a lot that other people would give anything to have—at the same time, it's a kind of cage you can't escape because you carry it with you all the time. When your face is all over some of the biggest grossing movies of your time, you can't escape your own celebrity.

I'd tried.

There had been a few awkward moments with Nova, but she seemed to have moved on, moved past my celebrity status. It was like she didn't care, like she didn't realize I was supposed to be different from everyone else.

I watched her take another careful sip. Her hand trembled slightly. "You're doing great," I said, mostly because it seemed like the kind of thing a nurse would say to encourage a patient.

She opened her eyes and peered at me. "I'll bet you say that to all the girls."

I laughed again. "It's my special technique for getting women with stomach flu to drink all their water."

"I'm sure." She smiled a shaky smile and pushed some limp hair from her eyes.

"Do you mind if I make myself at home in your kitchen?" I said, thinking I'd make myself some breakfast and maybe heat up some broth for her. Wasn't that what you gave sick people?

"Of course not. I'm going to stay here for now."

I patted her on the shoulder, the contact sending a shock of desire right to my groin. "Good enough. Make sure you drink all that water."

***

I realized my mistake when I got to the kitchen. The stove sat there, hulking huge and foreign-looking, and stared at me. Daring me to make it work.

I had no idea how to manage a wood-burning stove. I'd never even seen one like that before, one that looked like it belonged in a Western or something. Humiliating to admit I was at a loss. I was a guy, and guys were supposed to know all about manly things like heating a house with a wood fire.

After staring at the contraption for a few minutes, I poked around in its doors until I found the firebox. Nova had already started a fire in it, but it was dying a bit. At least, I thought it looked low, although I had no real idea what it was supposed to look like. I was from L.A. We didn't heat with wood in L.A.

I stuck another piece of wood in there to make sure the fire didn't go out. Then I located the wire gizmo Nova had used the other morning and stuck some bread in it to toast. She had eggs in her fridge. How hard could it be to scramble some eggs?

Half the eggs ended up getting burned onto her frying pan. The toast charred and I had to make more, but eventually I managed to produce a little food, which I brought to the table to eat. Just as I sat down, Nova appeared in the doorway.

"Did you set the house on fire?" she said, her lips curling up.

"Not yet, but I'm working on it."

"You should have waited for me."

I frowned at her. "You're sick. You should be laying on the couch or something."

Nova shook her head slowly, like it pained her. "You're my guest. It's my job to take care of you."

"Don't be stupid. Go lay down."

"You're such a charmer," she said with a roll of the eyes.

"Hey, I'm a big Hollywood star." I waggled my brows at her. "I know all the moves."

She laughed. It was weak and raspy, but I put that down to the fact she'd been vomiting all morning. It was a real laugh, and that was what counted. She clearly didn't hate me anymore.

Yeah, I know we'd already had that conversation, but I'd kept worrying about it. I'd imposed myself on her, even if it had been purely an accident, and she'd let me know. I wasn't used to that, wasn't used to feeling unwanted.

Jesus, I sounded like a whiny prick even to myself.

Enough self-pity. I looked at her and made shooing motions. "Go lay down. I'll bring you some more water in a sec."

"Fine. I'll lay down."

She stomped off to the living room in a mock temper. At least, I thought she was kidding me. It was hard to tell with her.

Chapter 18
Guitar

I found her on the couch later and set the water I'd brought on the end table, a pressboard and plastic piece of crap that looked like a relic of the seventies. She'd had another bout of vomiting while I cleaned up my breakfast mess, and now she looked utterly miserable. Didn't even open her eyes to look at me as I set down the glass.

"I hope you don't expect me to drink that," she said.

"Every drop, Miss Pennyman." I sat cross-legged on the floor next to the couch.

They had a cheap but attractive throw rug there, some kind of Oriental design in blue and red. Very traditional. The floor underneath was wooden planks, wide and clear-coated the natural color of the wood. I wondered how old the cabin was. It had a definite feeling of age to it.

Nova still wasn't drinking her water.

I tapped the glass. "You've got to drink something."

She groaned. "No."

"Just a little."

She opened one eye to glare at me. "I'll just puke again if I do."

"Funny, that's the same thing I said to you."

"Yes, and I'm deeply sorry for pestering you so much yesterday. Now will you please leave me alone?"

I thought about it for a second. "Nope. Can't do that."

"You're not going to get me to drink that water. Just so you know."

Okay, fine. Maybe she needed something to distract her from her misery. Maybe I could give her something else to be miserable about.

I glanced around the living room. There was a small bookcase crammed with paperbacks, two elderly club chairs, a fireplace ... and a guitar. The black guitar case stood propped in the corner next to the books, as if someone were trying to hide it.

I glanced at Nova, who looked like she was still trying to sleep. She wouldn't mind if I noodled around with her guitar, would she? I went over to the case and brought it to one of the chairs. When I opened it, I found a decent quality acoustic. Nice.

There was a tuner in the guitar case. Good thing, because I did not have perfect pitch. I gave Nova a furtive glance as I blew softly into the tuner to get a middle C.

Her head turned toward the sound. "What're you doing?"

"I'm gonna tune up this guitar, if that's okay."

"Oh, sure. Help yourself." She grimaced and put the water glass to her lips.

I tried not to grin at her. "Good girl; you're drinking your water."

"Yep, that's what I am. A good girl."

There was something a little bitter about that statement, but this wasn't the time to examine it. Anyway, it was none of my business. We weren't a couple. We would never be a couple.

Why did I have to keep telling myself that?

"I didn't know you played the guitar," she said as I continued tuning.

"Yeah, it's a hobby," I said.

"I haven't played in years."

"Oh, yeah? You any good?"

Nova shook her head with another grimace. "Not really."

"That's what you said about your art, too. You lied to me. And just for the record, I don't believe anything you say anymore."

"Whatever." She made a little huffing noise and pulled the throw blanket up to her chin.

I strummed some exploratory chords, just to get the feel of the instrument.

Maybe I was still sicker than I thought, because I was finding everything she did ridiculously cute. And that wasn't me. I didn't let women in, never got close to them. Friends, fine. I could do friends. And a quick lay was always good. But this combination of—of liking, affection, with hard lust. That was new and different. I had no idea what to do with it.

Besides, *he* could show up at any moment. I hadn't sensed the *presence* since I'd come to in her kitchen, but he couldn't be far. He never was. He probably already knew I was developing feelings for Nova and that would put her in danger.

No emotional involvement. That was my motto, but I wasn't sticking to the plan very well.

I chose a commonly played ballad for my first song, one of those soft lovey songs that metal bands put out every so often to get a female audience. It was something that was all over the radio and I was pretty sure Nova would recognize it. The lyrics were kinda sappy. Girls loved it.

"That's pretty," she said in a low voice when I finished. "What is it?"

I told her the name, surprised she didn't know it already.

"Did you write it?"

"No." I laughed a little. "It's by World Strider."

"Oh." She turned onto her back so she could look at me. "I told you I'm out of date. I don't know anything."

"Because you're so busy studying?"

"Yeah." She nodded, looking vaguely embarrassed.

"You know, most people I know are really busy, but they still know some of the popular songs," I said. "Do your parents lock you in a tower or something?"

"No." She frowned at me. "It's not like that. They just really want me to succeed. I want to succeed."

"Do you?"

"Yeah." She crossed her arms over her chest. "I do."

"Don't you ever make time to relax, though?" I said, strumming some random chords.

"Well, yeah. I guess." She frowned more deeply. "No, not really."

"That's messed up, Nova. You're too young to work all the time."

"I don't work all the time anymore. I'm on retreat, remember?"

"Okay, sure." I launched into an instrumental piece to forestall further conversation for a few minutes.

I'd been about to say something she wouldn't' want to hear. Her family pressures and life choices were none of my business, anyway. We weren't really friends, just strangers thrown together by weird circumstances. I had no right to offer my opinions or advice.

And these circumstances were definitely weird. Trapped in a cabin with a girl I'd ordinarily never give a second glance. Before I met her, I would've said she was definitely not my type. I watched her from under my lashes as I finished the piece and segued into another one. How could such an ordinary-looking girl be so beautiful at the same time?

There was something about her that just captured my attention and wouldn't let it go. Even when she was sick from stomach flu. I'd seen it the first instant I opened my eyes, although I couldn't explain what it was.

She had lovely features. She looked good without makeup, which was more than I could say for most of the women I'd hooked up with. But that wasn't it.

She was natural inside, too.

Nova didn't treat me like I was a member of another species. She didn't treat me like a celebrity, except for those few awkward moments after she'd accepted my real identity. She treated me like I really was just another regular guy.

I couldn't remember the last time I'd met a woman who did that, who wasn't also in show business.

I liked her in a way that had nothing to do with bagging her. And that was anything but normal for me.

What did that say about me and the fucked-up life I'd been living? Nothing good.

I knew there were people in the movies who didn't do drugs and sleep around. They existed. I'd worked with some of them. They'd never been part of my circle of so-called friends, though. I'd fallen in with Jeremy when we were both kid actors, and he'd already been experimenting with that shit.

Had Jer been a real friend or a so-called friend?

My body clenched all over and my fingers stumbled across the strings of the guitar. He and I had been buddies for so long and I'd never once asked myself that question. He was just Jeremy.

My throat closed up hard. It was a good thing I was still doing instrumental stuff because there was no way I could've sung through the pain in my throat. My voice would have come out all wobbly and distorted and I didn't want Nova to know what kind of shit I was thinking at the moment.

I still believed Jeremy was a real friend, in spite of his self-destructive side.

He'd befriended me when I was the know-nothing dumbass kid from the bad side of town. When I couldn't act my way out of a paper bag if I'd had a knife and a flashlight. He could've used my inexperience as an excuse to bully me. He could've ignored me, like so many of the others on that job had done. Instead he'd chosen to help me.

He'd never looked down his nose at me. He'd shown me around the set, helped me learn my lines, explained the business as only another kid could have done. In a way I could understand at the time.

He'd been at it years longer than I had.

Jeremy had been the first real, true friend I'd ever had. Maybe the only one. He'd just had a lot of problems of his own, and they'd gotten him in the end.

I segued from warming up to one of my favorite songs, ?. It had been a while since I'd played, and it felt good to let the music take over, drawing me away from my morbid inner monologue. Just letting it flow through me and the instrument, not thinking about anything, inhabiting the notes, the rhythm. It was a different kind of forgetfulness than acting.

I looked over at Nova when I finished the song. She was staring at me with open-mouthed astonishment. My face burned as I bent my head and studied the strings again.

"You're really good." She sounded surprised.

"Thanks." I was blushing, for chrissake. I could feel the heat in my face.

"I had no idea."

"You didn't even know who I was until I told you," I said.

"I'm sorry. I guess that was kind of insulting, huh?" She sounded more amused than sorry.

I glanced at her, then looked away. "No. It's fine."

"Gage. I can tell I hurt your feelings."

I scowled at her. "You did not hurt my feelings, Nova. I don't expect everyone in the world to know who I am or recognize me on sight. That would be ridiculous."

She smiled, an expression that made her look even more elfin than usual. "Okay. Would you play me something else?"

"Sure. What would you like to hear?"

"I have no idea. I don't know your repertoire."

"Repertoire?" I said, giving her an empty-headed stare. "That's an awful big word. What's it mean?"

She tossed a throw pillow at me. "Smartass."

I dodged. "Hey, careful there. You're going to damage the instrument."

"I'll damage the instrument all right. Now play something. Don't make me go over there."

"I'll play if you keep drinking your water. Otherwise, you get nothing." I pointed at the glass. "Drink up."

She heaved a theatrical sigh. "Fine."

I waited, eyebrows raised, until she took a sip.

"There," she said, glaring at me. "Satisfied now?"

"I'll be satisfied when the glass is empty."

I started another piece, "Raven's Beak" by World Strider, and didn't look up until it was done. When I checked, Nova was about a quarter of the way through the glass of water. This music thing was working. So I kept going, playing classics and some contemporary songs until she'd finished all of it.

"I love your voice," she said. Her face turned pink.

"Thank you. You're one of the few who's heard it."

"Really? You don't perform?"

"Hell, no."

She frowned. "Why not? You should. No, really, Gage. You're seriously talented."

"I don't know," I said. "It's just something I've always kept to myself. Except for Jeremy. We used to jam together sometimes."

"Jeremy?"

"Lindstrom. He—uh—he died last year." Stupid, but I still had trouble getting those words out of my throat.

"Oh. That's right; I remember hearing about that. It was really sad."

"Yeah." I tapped the sound box of the guitar. "Yeah, it was."

"I didn't know you were friends."

She didn't know a lot of things.

"We were pretty close," I said. I bent my head back to the guitar, strumming some random chords.

"It's hard to lose someone like that," she said softly.

"Yeah." I kept strumming.

"I had a friend who died when we were in high school."

"Oh, yeah?" I wasn't sure I wanted to hear about this.

"Yeah. She was riding her bike and she fell off. Hit her head. I guess she thought she was okay, because she just kept riding. But then she sort of fell over and passed out. And she died."

I looked over at her. She had a faintly sad, thoughtful expression on her face. Nothing to suggest she'd been deeply traumatized by the death, but sad anyway.

"Were you close to her?"

Nova shrugged. "Not super close. School friends. I wasn't there when it happened, but some other friends of mine were. They were really broken up. They blamed themselves, thought they should have known she was so badly hurt."

"Yeah," I said. "I guess that happens. People blame themselves."

"My mom told me it was really common. She's a GP and most of her patients are healthy, but she occasionally has patients who die."

"I—uh—I was there when Jeremy died. I mean, not when he died died, but when he ..." My voice trailed off. I cleared my throat. "What I mean is, I'm the one who found him."

She sat up a little straighter. "Oh, God. How awful."

"Yeah. Awful." I blew some air out through my nose and strummed a few more chords.

"He died of a drug overdose, right?" she said.

I nodded. "Yeah, he did." And maybe something else, but I couldn't tell her about that.

"I can't imagine how hard that must have been for you."

I hadn't really talked about it at all. Not with anyone. Nobody had wanted to hear about it.

Okay, that's not really true. Everyone had wanted to talk about it. Everyone had their opinion on what Jeremy's real problem had been, how his family and close friends should have helped him, or how nobody could have really helped him.

Everyone wanted the juicy, nasty details of his death. How had he looked, Gage? What was he doing at the time? Why do you think he chose that time to get wasted instead of waiting for you to show up? Do you think he meant to do it? Was it a suicide?

Or else they just looked at me like they thought I might explode at any moment. Or with pity. I hated that. The pitying glances and the whispers.

Gage found him, you know. He and Gage were supposed to go to a party together, you know. It must be eating Gage up inside ...

"You've probably talked it to death," Nova said.

"Not really."

"Oh?"

I glanced at her again. She didn't seem judgy. She was just watching me, her gaze calm but free of pity. Accepting, I guess. She seemed accepting.

"Yeah, everyone wanted to hear my side of it," I said. "But I really didn't feel like sharing. They just wanted the gossip. They didn't give a shit about Jer. Or me, either."

"So you didn't, like, see a counselor or anything? I thought everybody in L.A. was all about their therapists."

"Nope. That's New York."

She laughed. "Okay. I stand corrected."

"I didn't want to talk about it. I wanted to forget," I said. So why was I opening my mouth now?

"It seems like a tough thing to forget."

"It's impossible." Jer's dead gaze would be emblazoned on my brain for the rest of my life.

"You want to tell me?" Her voice sounded too even, like she was trying to keep the expression, the feeling, out of it.

"Nah, I'm good."

"Okay."

I looked across her, out the window. The snow still came down with pitiless intensity. I'd been in the mountains before, been to plenty of ski resorts, but I'd never seen a snowstorm like this one. We were going to have to dig ourselves out once it quit.

The snow made everything so quiet. Muted. Even the crackle of the fire in the kitchen stove seemed like its volume had been turned down. Like it was waiting for me to say something.

"He was in the tub."

"Jeremy?" she said.

"Yeah. That's where I found him." Jesus. I needed to keep my mouth shut, but it kept on moving, making words, in spite of my better judgment. "He'd been drinking Scotch. And there was a syringe in his arm."

"Shit."

"And some pills on the counter. The docs said there were a whole bunch of different drugs in his system." I didn't want to look at her, but my gaze made it over to her anyway. There wasn't any pity in her eyes. Just ... something else. Something I wasn't sure I could put a name to. "He was already cold. I touched him and his skin felt cold. His lips were blue. But his eyes were still open. It was really bizarre."

Yeah. Bizarre couldn't even touch how weird the scene had been.

"I'm so sorry, Gage." The strange thing was, she sounded like she meant it.

"Me too."

"Was that what you meant when you said you had some not-so-good friends?"

I shot her another wary glance. "Sort of. More the other ones, the people we used to hang around with."

"Like at the party? The one before you fell in the water?"

"Yeah. Like that." I'd made some boneheaded decisions in my life, mainly hanging around with the wrong people. And that was changing, as of now. I needed more people like Nova.

Jesus. What the hell was I thinking? More people like Nova would only mean good people getting hurt because of me.

I didn't deserve her, or anyone like her. My fame, my whole career, had been bought for me. Nothing I had was really mine; none of it was legitimate. The supernatural protection I'd had may have even cost my friend his life—at the very least, it had made him vulnerable to the pedophilic assholes who couldn't get me because of The Deal.

If I hadn't had The Deal hanging over me, protecting me, I would have been a target of the pedophiles in the business. I would have drawn attention away from Jeremy, at least to some degree. So he'd been molested and abused because of me.

It's not that I wished I'd been molested. Who would want something like that? Hell, no. But I'd had an unfair advantage over Jeremy. I hadn't deserved the extra protection I'd received. I got it through my mother's nefarious occult dealings. And that made it wrong.

Jeremy had suffered molestation because of me. He'd turned to drugs because of the molestation. And the drugs had killed him. Didn't that make me responsible, at least in part, for his death?

"Do you suppose they're looking for you?" Nova said, looking vaguely worried. "They must be wondering what happened to you. Maybe people think you're dead."

"Maybe they do." Right now I couldn't give a damn.

"I wish we had some way to call somebody. Let them know where you are."

I shook my head. "I think it's better this way. If people knew where I am, we'd be inundated with press. With fans. It would turn your cabin into a circus."

"Really? You think so?"

"Yep."

"They'd have trouble getting up here in this." She waved her hand in the direction of the window.

"True. But we don't have a working phone, so it's a moot point."

Nova's face suddenly contorted. She pressed a hand to her belly. "I—uh—I've gotta go." She bolted from the couch and staggered down the hall toward the bathroom.

Chapter 19
Shame

Gage wasn't playing the guitar anymore. Everything was embarrassingly silent as I locked myself into the bathroom. I opened the window a crack, just enough to let in some fresh air because honestly it didn't smell so good in there. The air that drifted in carried the scent of snow with it, cold and clean.

Yesterday, Gage had been the one suffering through this and I'd been the one on the outside. Now our positions were reversed.

I thought I'd been pretty cool about how sick he was. I thought I'd kept a polite distance. Now I understood that I'd been wrong. There couldn't be enough distance when something this mortifying was going on.

Stomach flu was the absolute worst thing ever. It should be outlawed. Nobody should have to go through this, and especially not when the world's most beautiful guy was right down the hall. If my mom had been here to help me, I wouldn't be ashamed. But with Gage ... it wasn't right. I didn't want him to know this was happening to me.

And he must have felt the same way when it was happening to him. No wonder he'd been so grouchy.

But what could we do? We both needed to stay in the cabin because of the storm. We were stuck together, mortifying illness or not. I guess we'd both have to pretend we didn't know or care what was going on. Or something.

Hey, you should feel privileged. Most people don't get to see Gage Dalton when he's sick.

Yeah. Yay, me.

He was an amazingly decent guy, once you got past the arrogant exterior. He'd been really sweet this morning, for example, so maybe I should feel privileged. I had the sense that he didn't show this side of himself to many people.

I finished up and hobbled back to the living room. He was picking out a tune on the guitar, humming softly to himself. He looked up and smiled at me as I made my way back to the couch and my heart fluttered helplessly.

He had the most stunning smile I'd ever seen. How did the women in his life stand it? The power of it was like, I don't know, almost like some kind of weapon. A weapon of pure male sexiness, to be deployed only with great care.

He set the guitar to the side and got up, stalking over to me with animal grace I hadn't seen in him until now. He'd probably been too sick before. Now all I could do was stare up at him as he prowled toward me. My heart was racing by this time.

What was he going to do? Would he sit with me? Did I want him to sit with me? I was still reeling from my bathroom embarrassment.

Yeah, I wanted him to sit with me. Maybe he'd hold my hand and comfort me. A girl could hope.

Gage reached for the side table and snagged my empty water glass. "I'll get you a refill."

I deflated as I watched him take the glass into the kitchen. He didn't feel the same way about me as I felt about him. That was clear. And why should he? I looked and probably smelled like a mess. Even on my best day, I was nowhere near his league.

A couple of minutes later, Gage came back with the glass. I put on my poker face. I wasn't going to let him know how much I liked him, how much I wanted him even when he needed a shower and was wearing my dad's old, faded black sweatpants and t-shirt.

They were too small for Gage, by the way. Like at least two sizes. Snug, that's what they were. It was a good look for him.

Poker face, Nova.

I looked out the window. As if I cared what the weather was doing. Please. I already knew it was still snowing and at this rate we'd be leaving via the upstairs windows when the storm was over.

The couch wiggled slightly. I froze for an instant as my heart zoomed out of control. He was sitting next to me. I could feel the press of his ass—hips, I mean hips—against my thighs.

There went the poker face.

"You need to drink some more," he said, sounding all concerned and caring.

I made myself look at him, smile like a normal person, and take the glass. "Thanks. You didn't have to do that."

"Yeah, I do. I owe you more than I could ever repay. So drink up." He gave me a stern look that I was pretty sure was fake.

I drank a tiny bit, just to please him, and sure enough I was rewarded with a smile. He was going to make me pass out if he kept looking at me that way.

It's not real. It's not real.

I needed to keep chanting that to myself, like a mantra. Maybe I'd become enlightened. Maybe not, but at least I wouldn't lose my heart to someone I had zero chance of keeping.

"Do you think you could eat something?" he said.

"Uh uh. No way. Don't even go there."

"Okay. Just thought I'd ask."

I managed another sip. "I've been wondering why nobody came around looking for you the day of your accident. I mean, this cabin is off the main road, but it's not totally hidden."

He shrugged, looking uncomfortable. "I didn't tell anyone I was leaving. And I parked my car off the road where it probably wouldn't be seen."

"Where was that?"

"The Mountain Magic Lodge and Cabins."

"Oh, that place. It went out of business this year. Why did you park there?" I didn't need to know, but I was curious.

"I saw the sign and thought they might have food. Then I got out to take a piss and like an idiot I fell in the water. The bank gave way."

"And you were alone?" I said, thinking of Blondie.

"Yeah. Why?"

I stared at the water glass. "This weird thing happened right before I found you. A guy came to my door. He told me his friend had fallen in the water and I needed to help him get you out. But when I went down to the river, he sort of disappeared."

Gage's gaze became disturbingly intent. "He disappeared? What do you mean?"

"I thought he was behind me. You know, following me down to the water? I asked him to help me pull you out, and when I turned around he was gone."

"Could he have walked away?"

I shook my head. "I don't think so. It was snowing, but he didn't leave any tracks. Besides, how would he know you were in the water if you were alone when you fell in? And he called you a friend. More than once."

He twisted his body so he faced me more fully. "What did he look like?"

"Tall. Skinny and blond. Long hair."

Gage went pale. "As tall as me? Hair down to his shoulders?"

"Yeah."

"That sounds like Jeremy." He rubbed his face. "Holy shit. I think you saw a ghost."

I thought back to the encounter. "You know, I noticed at the time that it was sleeting pretty hard but his hair wasn't getting wet. I thought it was odd."

He blinked rapidly and his mouth twisted. "Damn it," he said, his voice rough.

Without thinking, I reached out and laid my hand over his. It wasn't something I'd normally do with a guy I'd only met a couple days before, and as soon as our skin touched I blushed. But this was Gage—not the movie star but the guy I'd pulled from the river, the guy whose clothes I'd cut off, the guy I'd held naked just to keep him from dying.

Hand holding wasn't such a big thing next to all that.

His long fingers curled around mine. "He saved me. And I couldn't save him. Why didn't he just let me go?"

For an instant, I had no idea what to say. He really thought his best friend should have let him die?

"He obviously cared a lot about you," I managed.

Gage snorted. I didn't like the way he looked. Almost angry, as if he hated himself or something.

"Hey," I said. "What's that about?"

He shook his head without speaking.

"I'm glad he came to me," I said.

Still, he gave me nothing.

I squeezed his hand. "Gage, are you okay? You're starting to worry me."

"No." He frowned. "Don't worry about me." He turned a troubled gaze to me. "I don't want you to ever worry about me, okay?"

"But—"

"Promise me, Nova. Tell me you won't worry about me."

"I—I can't do that. I might not be able to help it."

"You have to."

"But why? Why are you saying this?" He was outright scaring me now. I didn't like the undercurrent of self-loathing I could hear in his voice. Didn't like it one bit.

"Never mind." He sighed and gave me a weak grin. "I guess I'm just tired. I'm not making any sense."

He was trying to change the subject and doing a poor job of hiding it. You'd think an actor would be able to fake it with ease, but maybe real-life lies were different from acting on-screen.

"Look," I said. "I'm not going to promise not to care or worry about you. Sorry, but it's too late for that. I started caring the second I saw you floating in the river. I can see you're upset about something and if you don't want to talk about it, that's okay. I'm not going to bug you."

"I'm sorry. I just don't think I can talk about it."

I was stupidly disappointed. Some part of me must have hoped he'd bare his soul to me, that I was special enough that he would talk to me when he hadn't with anyone else. Silly, silly girl.

"Okay," I said, and lifted the water glass to my lips to hide my reaction.

"Thanks for understanding," he said. "It's more important for you to drink that than listen to me whine all day anyhow."

I didn't think he was whining. He cared about his friend and missed him and seemed to be carrying around some kind of survivor's guilt or something. I wished I could take some of that burden from him, but if he didn't want to talk to me there was nothing I could do.

"Drink your water, Nova."

"Yes, Dr. Gage." I drank obediently.

My stomach still hurt. Getting the water down was difficult and all I could do was wet my tongue, over and over. Swallowing an actual mouthful would have sent me back to the toilet.

I kept sipping to please him and because I knew it was the right thing to do. But my mind kept traveling back and forth over everything he'd told me. I kept remembering the blond man who'd led me to him. Had it really been Jeremy Lindstrom's ghost?

I had no rational explanation for the lack of footprints. He'd been right behind me. There should have been footprints. But why had the thought of Jeremy helping him upset Gage so much?

He seemed almost to blame himself for Jeremy's death, which made no sense to me. I kind of got the whole guilt thing, but honestly what could he have done? If Jeremy had wanted to kill himself with drugs, he'd do it and nobody could really prevent it. Besides, maybe he'd just misjudged his dose. He'd been mixing drugs. What could Gage have done to stop him from doing that?

I wasn't trying to be callous toward Jeremy. I just thought Gage was taking on way too much responsibility for his friend's problems. Unless he provided the drugs or helped Jeremy inject himself, I couldn't see how he could be at fault.

Maybe there was something about Gage that I didn't know, something that would explain his sense of guilt.

Chapter 20

Kiss

Bathing in water that's just a degree warmer than a glacier isn't much fun, but it's better than going without. At least that's what I told myself the next afternoon as I dumped a pan of the stuff over my hair. There was a hot water reservoir on the stove, but I'd had to split the water in it between Gage and me, so neither of us got anything warm. Just less icy.

We'd both gone a couple of days without bathing and we were desperate. Being both sick and dirty gets old really fast, and now that I wasn't vomiting anymore I wanted to be clean.

I toweled off and stuck my dry, clean clothes on as quickly as possible. Then I went to the master bedroom and stuck my head in the doorway. Gage had already taken his bath and was on the bed, his eyes closed. He looked as exhausted as I felt. I needed to leave him alone so we could both get the rest we needed.

"Hey," I said softly.

His eyes opened. "Hey yourself."

"I'm going up to the loft to take a nap."

He patted the mattress next to his body. "Stay here with me so you don't have to climb the ladder."

He wanted me in bed with him?

I was probably just a warm body, something comforting while he stayed here. Maybe he was bored. But honestly I didn't care. This was an opportunity I couldn't bring myself to pass up, and thank God I'd remembered to brush my teeth first.

"Okay." I sat gingerly on the edge of the mattress.

Poker face, Nova.

"Come here." He looped a heavy arm around my waist and drew me down next to him. He sighed against my hair. "You feel good."

So do you.

"Um ... thanks."

"I really like you, Nova. I'm trying not to, because I'm not a good guy. You shouldn't get involved with me."

He wanted to be involved? With me?

"I think you're a good guy," I said, turning around to face him.

Gage was just as overwhelming up close as he was from across the room. Okay, he was twice as overwhelming. It really wasn't fair to the rest of us mortals that men like him roamed the earth, looking so unbelievably gorgeous while they did it. I mean, talk about an unfair advantage.

He frowned at me. "I'm not. I'll hurt you, and I don't want to do that."

"If you weren't a good guy, you wouldn't care if you hurt me," I said. Eminently logical. That's me.

"Sometimes I can't—there are things you don't know about me. Things I can't tell you. They're bad and they could get you hurt."

He looked so damned serious telling me this. It made me wonder about those not-so-good friends of his. Was he involved with drug dealers or something?

I reached up and touched his face, skimming my fingertips along his cheekbone. "I don't expect anything from you. We've only known each other a few days. There's no need to get all stressed about this, right?"

The frown deepened. "You don't expect anything from me?"

His skin felt surprisingly smooth until I let my fingertip wander down to where his beard was starting to come in. "You're not going to be here long, right? You're just visiting. After you go, we'll probably never see each other again. So don't worry about hurting me."

"I thought you said you cared about me," he said with a wry twist of his mouth.

"I do. But that doesn't mean I think I have some kind of hold on you. I know I don't."

I guess I'd expected him to feel relief that I wasn't making demands on him. I was telling him he could kiss me, maybe do more, and I'd be okay with him leaving. But he didn't respond at all the way I expected.

"I get the feeling you're trying to let me down easy," he said.

"What? No, I'm not. Why would you think that?"

"You're different. You never do what I expect. And I don't know how to read you."

"Like this." And I leaned up and kissed him.

It was just a soft press of the lips. Not much of a kiss, really. But my pulse raced and my sex pulsed with liquid heat and my mind boggled that I'd had the audacity to kiss someone like him at all.

A big, male hand instantly slipped behind my neck as his mouth opened on mine. He sucked on my lower lip, then my upper, then back to the lower. I nipped him and he moaned and his tongue licked me, asking for entry.

I gave it to him. He tasted like toothpaste and something else, something male that had me pressing my whole body up against him.

His leg hooked around one of mine and his arm tightened around my waist.

And suddenly he was kissing me like he needed me in order to breathe.

Every nerve in my body lit up. The hot, wet slide of his tongue, the hard heat of his body against mine, the taste of him, the pressure of his hand on my ass—all of it had me moaning and undulating against him as my core contracted in yearning. He massaged my ass, making me whimper.

I'd never reacted to Barry this way. Nobody had ever made me light up the way Gage did. Until now, I hadn't even known it was possible.

His hand slid upward, then beneath my waistband and inside my panties. "Is this all right?" he murmured against my lips.

"Yeah," I whispered back.

His fingers brushed my damp folds. I cried out at the burst of pleasure.

He drew his finger along first one crease and then another, making me squirm and whimper and moan. Our mouths continued to mate—and that was the only word for what they were doing. We made love with our mouths, our tongues, as he explored my pussy.

I trembled. My hands clutched at him. He pushed a single finger inside my body and my eyes rolled back as I gave another cry. Everything in me desired him, needed him, longed for him. When he bent his finger inside me, I came apart, grinding my pelvis against his hand.

Bursts and flashes of ecstasy bloomed in my core. I couldn't kiss him anymore. All I could do was shout and groan through my orgasm.

When the explosions died away, I still trembled. Gage rested his forehead against mine. He was breathing heavily.

"Damn, baby," he said. "That was incredible. You're incredible."

"I didn't do anything," I said, my voice trembling.

He laughed softly. "Oh, yeah, you did."

I could feel the bulge of his erection pushing against my thigh and I reached down between us to cup him. "Let me take care of you now."

He groaned, pulling his hips away. "No. Not a good idea."

"Why not?"

"It just isn't. For all the reasons I already told you."

"But that's not fair to you."

"It's fair, believe me." He pressed a finger to my lower lip. "You're the sexiest woman I've ever known. But this can't go any further."

Earlier, he'd said I was trying to let him down easy, but it seemed to me that he was the one doing the rejecting. Except he'd just had his hand down my panties, so maybe not. This terrible secret of his really sucked.

"Let's get some sleep," he said. "We're both still pretty sick."

"I don't think I'm going to be able to sleep after that," I said. I wanted to climb on top of him and have my wicked way with him.

"I'm sorry. I wish I could give you more." He really did sound regretful.

I fought back a sigh and tried to be cool about it. "It's all right. I understand."

Except I didn't. Not at all.

Chapter 21

Hot

Gage:

Nova fell asleep almost instantly. I lay next to her, propped up on my elbow and aching with unrequited lust, and watched her for a while. This stomach bug was kicking our butts, and she still looked sick despite her bath.

But she was so damn beautiful—pale, elfin face, thick black lashes, perfectly shaped lips.

It felt surreal, lying in bed with this gorgeous woman and not doing anything sexual with her. I still had the scent of her pussy all over my hand, but at the moment we weren't fooling around. She was sleeping, for chrissake.

I never slept with women. Never let them sleep with me.

What was I doing here? I was going to get her in trouble. I should haul my ass off the bed and go sleep on the couch, but I couldn't bring myself to do it.

I brushed a long strand of dark hair off her face. She smiled in her sleep, and turned to snuggle into me. Damn. My arm slipped around her as a whole new feeling of warmth flooded my chest.

I was falling for her. And that was just all kinds of wrong, as a character I'd once played would have said.

Since we were stuck here and I was almost as wiped out as she was, I closed my eyes and settled in for a nap. Yet I knew I couldn't let this thing between us continue. For her sake, I had to put some walls between us.

***

When I woke up, something felt wrong. Nova still slept beside me, so it wasn't that. There was something in the air...

No, there was a lack of something in the air. It was freezing cold outside the nest of blankets and bodies we'd made. I could feel it biting at my cheeks and nose.

Shit. Nova must have forgotten to put wood in the stove and the fire must have gone out. Somebody had to get it going again, and that somebody was me. There was no way I was going to wake Nova up when she was sleeping so well.

I slid out of bed. She didn't even move a finger.

In the kitchen, I found a single piece of firewood next to the stove. When I opened the firebox, I found nothing but a big pile of fluffy, gray ash. Great. City boy was going to have to figure out how to light a fire in that thing.

I could do this. But first I had to get some snow-worthy clothes so I could haul in more firewood.

Sneaking back into the bedroom, I rummaged through the closet and dresser as quietly as I could to see if I could turn up any more men's clothing. I found nothing but more ancient T-shirts and sweatpants. Her dad seemed to have a love affair with the things.

I ended up with three layers of T-shirt and two pairs of sweatpants. Hey, it was cold out there and I didn't have a coat. Nova had cut my red jacket into pieces getting it off me.

At least my shoes were whole and dry.

Outside, the snow still fell. It seemed to be coming down a little slower, but not by much. I tried to push the back door open and found it blocked by a foot of the stuff. I grabbed the shovel she had propped next to the door. I'd have to dig my way out.

The good thing about digging is it heats up your body and makes the cold easier to tolerate. The bad part—at least for me—was I had no idea where I was supposed to go. Where was her woodpile?

I stood in the narrow lane I'd created from her door down her back steps, my arms cold and wet from melting snowflakes, and scanned the yard. There was a long, narrow lump on the other side that could be the right spot, so I aimed for that and started digging.

It seemed like hours before I had a clear path and could start hauling the wood. My fingers were starting to go numb and I was exhausted. The damned stomach flu was still ruling me, but I wasn't going to let it win. We had to stay warm or we could both die.

Finally I had what I thought was enough wood in the house. It took up a giant chunk of the kitchen floor and I surveyed it with satisfaction. That ought to do for now.

I chose a few pieces off the top and stuck them in the firebox, then lit a match and threw it in too. The match fizzled and went out without making so much as a scorch mark on the wood.

I sighed, feeling like an idiot. I'd never done any of this outdoor stuff. As a kid, I'd been too busy making movies and none of them had been about survival in a snowstorm. I'd been too busy and too famous to do anything normal like join Boy Scouts. How the fuck did you start a fire, anyway?

Then I remembered you were supposed to start with tinder or something like that. Something small and easy to burn.

Scanning the room again, I noticed a sizable pile of old newspapers in a box along the wall near the stove. I almost face-palmed. How could I have missed that? I grabbed a handful of the stuff and started wadding up the pages.

It turns out you need a lot of tinder to start a fire with wet wood ... and a lot more tinder to keep it going. I ended up having to set some pieces on the stove top to dry them out before they'd burn.

"Um ... what are you doing?" Nova said.

I spun around to see her standing in the doorway, a quizzical smile on her face.

"I got some wood."

"Yeah, I see that." Her smile deepened. "Looks like enough for at least a week."

It was good to see her smiling like that. Our session in the bedroom hadn't made her afraid of me or embarrassed as far as I could tell.

"It was cold in here," I said. "And the fire had died."

"You got it going again?"

I gave her a mock-stern glare. "I don't like your tone of surprise. I'll have you know I've got mad backwoods skillz."

She laughed. "Okay. Well, thanks for getting in all that wood. It's a really impressive pile. Did you leave any outside?"

"I'm just not appreciated around here." I shook my head regretfully.

Nova came over, pressed her front to me, and stuck her hands in my sweatpants pockets. "I appreciate you more than you know," she purred.

Instant hard-on. She had no idea how she affected me ... although the bulge in my pants might have given her a clue. I growled and grabbed her ass, bending my head down for a kiss.

And then I ruined everything by swaying on my feet as my vision went black around the edges.

"Gage? Are you okay?" Nova sounded scared. "Oh my God, what's wrong?"

"Nothing," I said thinly as I fought for balance. "But I may have overdone it slightly."

"Go lay down on the couch."

"Nah, I'll be all right."

"Lay down." Now she sounded like the Dr. Pennyman I remembered from my first encounter with her.

"You're sicker than I am," I said.

"I didn't shovel snow and haul firewood. Go lay down. I'll bring you some tea in a few minutes." She punctuated her sentence with a light shove to my chest.

"I'm not letting you wait on me when you're sick." I closed my eyes to stop the spinning the room was doing.

"I won't collapse from making tea. Go on. Lay down or I'll pitch a fit like you've never seen."

I opened my eyes a slit and peered down at her. She was frowning at me. Was she really worried about me?

"Okay," I said grudgingly. "I'll go. But you take it easy." I let go of her ass.

"Go before you fall down. If you fall, I won't be able to pick you up."

She had a point there. I shuffled into the living room and sank onto the couch. I hated being sick, hated showing weakness, and hated depending on someone who should have been able to depend on me instead. But Nova was right. If I fell down and couldn't get back up, I'd be stuck on the floor because she sure as hell couldn't carry me. And I wouldn't do that to her.

She came back in the promised few minutes with tea for both of us. I pulled my legs up to make room for her on the couch and she sat down with me. Her arm brushed my leg.

"You're wet," she said.

"Yeah, I got snow all over my pants."

She made an impatient sound. "Go get something dry on. No, don't. Stay there and I'll bring it to you."

"Nova—"

"Not another word, Dalton." She set down her tea mug and walked toward the bedroom.

Was it wrong that I kinda liked her taking care of me? Even when she bossed me around. That was sort of hot, actually. We could work with it.

She came back with dry pants. "Do you need help getting them on?"

"No way. I'll do it myself." I stood up, a little unsteadily, and took them from her.

"Okay, if you're sure." She seemed to be hiding a smile.

"I'm sure." I shoved the wet pants down my legs.

Chapter 22

Not Art

Nova blushed a brilliant pink and turned away as I bared myself in the middle of her living room. I grinned. After what we'd done together, and the way she'd touched me, I hadn't thought I would embarrass her by undressing.

"I—uh—I really would like to see some of your movies," she said, transparently attempting to change the subject.

"Would you?"

I willed myself not to be flattered by her interest in my work. She was probably only trying to be polite—and change the subject. Besides, my work was just what I did. It wasn't that special. Anyone who could memorize lines could do what I did.

"Yeah," she said. "I mean, you're—well—yeah." She ended with a vague arm gesture.

"If you give me your address, I'll send you copies," I said. "After I get home."

"Okay."

I kicked off the wet pants and somehow got into the dry ones, although I was swaying again and my vision seemed unstable. Finally, they were on and I could flop back on the couch. "I'm decent now," I said.

She turned around and took the seat she'd abandoned. "Have you been in a lot of movies?"

"Yeah, I guess." I shrugged. "I've kinda lost count." I rattled off the titles of a few of my pictures.

"I haven't seen any of those." She sighed. "I'm sorry."

I leaned my head against the arm of the couch and pulled the throw blanket over myself. "Don't be sorry."

"But you've been in so many and I haven't even seen one. It feels like an insult to your art or something."

"My art?" I snorted. "It's not art, believe me. I don't know why people insist on tagging me as an artist, because I sure as hell don't deserve it."

"What?" She narrowed her eyes at me. "Why would you say that?"

"I didn't earn any of it," I said, thinking of The Deal. "It was all given to me. I've just been along for the ride."

Her head tilted as she studied me. "I don't get it. How was it given to you? You're not related to any big Hollywood names, are you? So you didn't get in by nepotism."

"No, it's just—forget it." I waved it off. "I'm just tired and I don't know what I'm talking about."

I couldn't tell her. She'd think I was a lunatic. Jeremy's ghost was one thing. Lots of people have seen a ghost or two. But deals with the devil? That's a problem you don't hear about every day, and Nova with her science background would never believe me.

Besides, I'd always had the feeling that if I told anyone, that person would suffer. I don't even know where the idea came from originally. It seemed like it had always been with me, every time I made a new friend, every time I got close to revealing the truth about my life.

I picked up my tea mug, my hands trembling slightly from exhaustion, and sipped. She'd really sugared the hell out of it and it tasted pretty good.

"I think you're too hard on yourself," she said. "And I don't know why you'd think you didn't earn your career. It's not like someone else starred in those movies. That was all you, right?"

I sighed. "Nova, let's just drop it, okay? I really don't want to talk about it."

She gave me her Dr. Pennyman look. "I don't like to hear you putting yourself down."

"I'm not."

"Yeah, you are. You're totally devaluing your acting."

I crossed my arms over my chest. "You haven't even seen any of my acting. How do you know I'm any good?"

"You must be pretty good or you wouldn't be so successful."

I laughed and shook my head. She was so naive in some ways. "That's not necessarily true."

"Well, I'm going to watch all of them and give you my assessment." She raised her brows at me. "And you'll accept it. Right?"

"Yes, ma'am."

She smirked. "That's better."

I wished I could tell her everything. The only other person in the world who knew was my mom, and we couldn't have a rational conversation about it. The thing is, I didn't want to endanger Nova just so I could get shit off my chest.

Maybe we could talk around the edges of the problem, though.

"Have you ever been tied into something you hated because of what someone else did?" I said.

Nova tilted her head again. "Um ... yeah, I guess. What exactly do you mean?"

I shrugged. "You know, just, some kind of responsibility you wouldn't have taken on, except this other person has saddled you with it. And now you can't get out of it."

She studied me, and I had an awkward yet exhilarating feeling that she could actually see inside my mind. "My pre-med major is kind of like that," she said slowly. "My parents want me to be a doctor and just recently I realized I've only been going through with it because of them."

"But you're not tied to it, right? You can back out."

Her beautiful mouth twisted. "Technically, yeah. But how do you tell your parents you want to disappoint them?"

"You hate the idea of becoming a doctor?"

"I think it would make me miserable," she said.

"Then tell them that. I'm sure they want you to be happy."

She wasn't getting it, but then how could she? Her situation wasn't remotely like mine. I sympathized with her about her insistent parents, but it was hardly in the same league as my mom's deal with Old Nick.

What would happen if I gave up acting? If I tried to fade into the background, just be normal? *He* would probably come storming into my life to fuck with my friends for real and maybe kill me as well. Because my giving up wasn't part of the The Deal.

"I'm getting the feeling," Nova said, "that your problem is a lot deeper than mine."

"Yeah," I said with a lift of one shoulder. "It sort of is."

"Can you tell me about it?"

"No. I'm sorry." God, I hated the way she was looking at me. Like I'd disappointed her or something. Disappointing Nova hurt me, just like the way she was looking at me hurt. I was turning into a pussy.

"It's like—say someone had signed you up for military service, maybe," I said after an awkward pause. "Something really intense that you didn't want to do and couldn't possibly escape. At least, not without dying and getting other people hurt too."

She frowned, squinting at me and pursing her lips. "I can't even imagine what that might be."

"Just go with it. What if somehow you were drafted into some elite military unit and you didn't want to be there but you had to go forward no matter what it did to you? Even if you had to do some bad shit and you didn't know if you could live with that?"

She blew out a heavy breath and leaned against the couch back. "I don't know. I guess—I guess I'd be mad as hell. And I'd be looking for a way out."

"There is no way out."

"How do you know that?" Those honey-gold eyes of hers were so serious. "Have you ever tried?"

Well, no. I'd assumed. I'd gone with what my mother had told me. Why had I done that?

"I trusted the person who got me into the mess," I said after another long silence.

"Maybe you shouldn't have trusted them. After all, they're the one who did it to you."

"Yeah. Isn't that the truth."

"Have you told anyone else about this? Maybe someone would have an idea of how to help you."

I shook my head. "No. No way. If I talk about it, the person I tell could get hurt."

"You're starting to scare me," she said, her tone apprehensive.

I met her gaze. "You should be scared, Nova. This is dangerous stuff."

She put her hand on my calf and squeezed. "I just wish you would tell me anyway. I want to help you."

"I wish I could, but I wouldn't be able to stand it if you got hurt."

"There's got to be something we can do."

She leaned against my shin, put her arm around my thigh and laid her cheek against my propped-up knee. I stroked her hair. I couldn't picture anyone else I knew taking my part the way she had. She was so generous. Too generous for her own good.

"Is this why you told me not to worry about you?" she said softly.

"Yeah."

"It's too late, you know."

"Yeah, you told me." I kept stroking those long, dark locks. "But I'd like you to try anyway. I don't want to hurt you. Ever."

"Well, whatever it is that's threatening you can't find us up here, right? I mean, we're in the middle of nowhere, in a huge snowstorm. Even if they knew where you were, they wouldn't be able to reach you."

If only that were true. I kept petting her hair while saying nothing.

It wasn't her fight and I didn't want her getting involved. I'd already said too much as it was. The thought of getting some outside help was tempting, but I couldn't go there. This was something I had to do on my own, because I didn't want anyone else getting hurt.

When I was in my teens, I'd tried to talk to my mom about it. About getting out of The Deal. She'd gotten hysterical, started screaming and carrying on about how I'd ruin everything and kill everyone I knew, and then gone on a week-long drinking binge. That was the last time I'd attempted that kind of conversation.

The notion of getting out of The Deal hadn't even occurred to me again until the past few months. I'd been so caught up in my career, in the busy-ness of it, all the demands, that it hadn't crossed my mind. Plus, The Deal had been part of the background of my life since I was ten, so in a way it was all I knew. Then Jeremy had died.

Maybe I could do my own research. Maybe there was a way out there somewhere and I could find it on my own. It was worth a try.

But would I really kill my friends if I did? Would *he* take them in retribution?

Chapter 23
Supernatural

Nova:

I loved the way he was stroking my hair. It wasn't sexual, not really, but there was something so intimate about it. The dimly lit living room and the silence brought by all the snow outside made it feel even more tender. As if it meant something, even though it was just an idle gesture on his part.

Whatever was bothering Gage, I could tell it was serious. It just sounded so bizarre. From the little he'd told me, it was no ordinary problem. It didn't even sound like the mob.

Okay, it sort of did sound like the mob, but I had a powerful hunch that organized crime had nothing to do with it. But what else could it be?

He seemed almost haunted. Which was ironic, considering that his ghostly friend had led me to him in the first place.

Maybe he really was haunted. Maybe he didn't want to tell me because he thought I'd laugh at him. Or maybe he really did believe that whatever this thing was would come after me once I knew about it.

Of course, I knew about it now. Not the details, but its existence—of that I was aware. And it was one of those cat out of the bag problems— once the cat was out, there was no way you were getting it back in. What has been seen cannot be un-seen. You couldn't un-know something like this.

Yeah. Whatever this is.

"Gage, you know I would never laugh at you, right? I mean, sure, I teased you this morning, but I would never really laugh at you. You can tell me anything, I swear it."

He gave me a weary smile that sat oddly on his youthful face. "Thanks, Nova. It means a lot to me to hear you say that. But it wouldn't be right for me to involve you."

"I don't understand. How could this thing or person get to me? Nobody knows about me. If you don't tell and I don't tell, how could they possibly find out?"

"Oh, they can find out anything. Believe me."

"You know what this sounds like, right?"

"He shook his head. "No, what?"

"It sounds supernatural."

He laughed. "Nah. It's nothing that interesting."

I watched him through narrowed eyes. "Really?"

"Yeah, really. It's totally mundane. Just in a really dangerous way."

"Okay," I said, not sure if I believed him.

"You're doubting me."

My eyes opened wide. "No, I'm not." I so was.

"Fine," he growled.

"Fine."

He glowered at me. "I didn't think you believed in the supernatural."

I shrugged. "I did see Jeremy's ghost, remember?"

"Yeah, but with your parents being doctors, I figured—"

"First of all, my parents aren't me," I said with some asperity. "Second, even doctors can have otherworldly experiences. Even doctors' kids."

He raised his brows, a much more relaxed look coming over him. "Oh, yeah? Want to tell me about it?"

"No. You can't be involved. It's too dangerous."

He tossed a pillow at me. "Not funny, Pennyman. And you promised me you would never laugh at me."

"Oops. Sorry. I wasn't thinking."

He nudged me with his foot. "So give. What did you see?"

Biting my lip, I considered whether I wanted to tell him. Not that I thought I couldn't trust him. But I didn't talk about this stuff either. Not normally, anyway. Most of my friends would have thought I'd lost my marbles if I did.

I licked my lips. "Okay. Well, it wasn't something I saw. It was something I heard."

"Oh."

Oh? That was all he had to say?

"Go on," he said.

I took a deep breath. "I heard my friend calling for me. The one who died. Remember I told you about her?"

"I remember."

"Yeah, the day she died, I was studying in my room and I heard her voice calling my name. It was clear and it sounded exactly like she was in the room with me. But she was several miles away."

"Weird."

"Yeah. I actually never told anyone about this."

"Why do you suppose she called for you? You said you two weren't all that close."

"I don't know. Maybe because my parents are doctors? I wondered the same thing."

Gage looked thoughtful. "Did you ever hear her voice after that?"

"No. Not ever once." I looked him right in the eye. "But I believe in ghosts and spirits now. No matter what anybody says. I know because I've experienced it. So you really can talk to me and I won't laugh."

I so wanted him to confide in me. To be honest, my curiosity was driving me wild. But I also wanted to see if I could help him. He seemed so alone, and not just because he was stuck in this cabin with only me for company. There was something essentially alone about him, like he'd never really had a true friend. Like there was no-one in his life in whom he could confide. No-one to trust.

That seemed awful to me.

He only sat up straighter and leaned in for a kiss. "You're amazing, Nova. If I told anyone, it would be you. But I'm serious about the danger. I don't want you to get hurt ever, and especially not because of me. I think it would kill something in me if you got hurt."

He was cupping the side of my face and I laid my hand over his. I turned my head and kissed his palm. "I wish you didn't have to go."

"So do I."

"Really? You really wish you could stay with me?"

"Yeah. I do." He smiled wryly. "Did you think I was lying?"

"No. But it's so hard for me to believe me. I mean, look at me. You're—well, you're you, and I'm just plain old Nova."

"Jesus, Nova, there is nothing plain about you. Not one thing. You're one of the most beautiful women I've ever met. I mean that, so quit looking at me that way. Most of the women I know require at least an hour of work and a ton of makeup to look as good as you do with a bare face."

My face started to burn. His words were sweet, but they couldn't be true. How could I compete with all those Hollywood beauties?

"And your personality is beautiful too."

"You're a sweet talker," I said.

"Not really. You want to know the truth?"

I nodded.

"Usually women throw themselves at me. I don't really have to work at this stuff. They seek me out. They follow me around, try to arrange meetings, shit like that. It's embarrassing sometimes. But it makes it easy for me. Maybe too easy."

His beautiful face looked completely guileless and I felt I could believe him. But part of me wondered if I were being played. He knew how ignorant I was of Hollywood goings-on, so he could feed me all kinds of bullshit and I'd never know the difference.

I wanted to believe him, though.

"I know you hear this all the time," I said, my hand still over his, "but you're beautiful too. And not just on the outside."

Gage Dalton actually blushed. He ducked his head as his cheeks turned pink.

"Thanks, Nova. I think you're just flattering me, but thanks."

"I am not flattering you. It's true." I leaned over his bent knee to kiss him on his beautiful mouth. "How many guys would be as protective of me as you've been? Not many, I can tell you. How many guys would make themselves sick getting the firewood in so I wouldn't have to do it?"

"Come on, any guy would've done the same thing."

"I don't think so. Maybe a few pieces, an armload or something, but not the whole woodpile."

"I thought you said you wouldn't laugh at me," he said, his lips curling up at the corners.

"I'm not."

A sideways glance. "You so are."

"Nope. I thought it was really touching. But I don't want you doing it again, because if you die on me I'll have to kill you."

He laughed a little. "I wouldn't want that."

"Nobody does, believe me."

Chapter 24
Want

I tried, sometimes subtly and sometimes not so subtly, to get Gage to confess to me over the next two days. But he wouldn't. He never opened up to me about it again, just flat out refused to talk about it. I'd never known anyone so stubborn.

Damn it. The more I pondered what it could be, the more I wanted to know. But I couldn't force him to tell me.

It had been two days since Gage kissed me. We hadn't talked about it and we hadn't done it a second time. We were both pretending it had never happened as we sat at the kitchen table and ate together.

I took our dinner plates to the sink for washing. Crumbs of the omelets I'd made still clung to their shiny white surfaces. Gage followed me. I could feel his gaze on my back; it made me hot and nervous with self-conscious anticipation.

Did he still want me? Why had he stayed so distant since the kiss?

We'd talked, sure, but just as friends. We'd played music and I'd made a couple of pictures of him. Yet we hadn't touched beyond our fingers accidentally brushing.

I turned on the water and soaped up a dish cloth.

"Let me help with that." His voice came so close to my ear that he startled me.

I jumped, making him chuckle.

"You can dry." I pointed to the drawer that held my towels.

He grabbed a towel. When he stood next to me, he chose a spot so close his hips almost touched mine. I could feel the heat from his body through the sweatshirt I wore and it made my heart trip a little.

I washed the first plate, rinsed it, handed it to him. Our hands touched. I swallowed hard and picked up the second plate. When I gave it to him, our hips bumped.

"Sorry," I squeaked.

He grinned down at me and bumped me again. "I don't mind."

Oh. He didn't? Confusion and a hot blush covered me as I rinsed my hands and the sink. Gage dried the second dish and put it in my dish rack, watching me the whole time out of the corner of his eye.

He reached out and stroked the upper plane of my cheekbone. "Nova."

I looked up at him, heart pounding now. "Gage?"

114

He took me in his arms. My heart instantly began to pound and my core heated and throbbed. We hadn't done anything more than kiss since that first time, but kissing was all it took for me to get excited when I was with him. Sometimes I didn't even need the kissing.

I set my hands at his tight and narrow waist and nuzzled my face against his chest. He smelled like my soap, but he smelled like himself too, and that was something I'd never tire of.

It was a little scary, how powerfully I was attracted to him. What would happen when he went home? It was going to hurt. A lot.

He tipped up my chin with his forefinger and leaned down to brush his lips against mine. He'd gotten even better at kissing me, something I would never have thought possible. It was like he'd learned me, just from that, and could now push every one of my sexual buttons.

I sighed against his mouth as he licked my lower lip. Barry never affected me the way Gage does and I wasn't quite sure how to handle it. I mean, my whole body almost hurt because I wanted him so much and that wasn't something I'd ever experienced. What do you do with that?

So I looped my arms around his shoulders because he was too tall for me to reach his neck, but then he bent down nearer to me and I could finally reach his neck and I stroked the skin there and it was so smooth and warm and I wanted to kiss it. I wanted to kiss every part of him. That was something else I'd never experienced—wanting to kiss a man's skin, touch him, do things to him. Before, I'm sorry to say, I'd always been a bit passive.

His hands, big and warm, covered my ass and kneaded my flesh and there was something weirdly erotic about that. It made me moan into his kiss. And my moan seemed to excite him. he squeezed me harder as his tongue plunged deeply into my mouth, giving me a powerful taste of him. I clutched him. I slid my tongue over his, pushed it along the smooth hard ridge of his teeth. I took his lower lip between my teeth and pulled.

We'd kissed before, but only the first time had been truly passionate like this. He'd been holding out on me.

One of his hands slid from my ass to my waist. He left it there for a moment. Then up it went, up my torso, along my rib cage, until his thumb rested just below the curve of my breast. I panted against his mouth, wanting him to touch me there. Even for an instant. I just wanted his hand on me. So much.

His thumb rubbed back and forth along the under-curve of my breast and my heart pounded even harder, faster. The hard bulge in his pants pressed against my lower belly, clear proof of his real desire for me. I liked that. I liked it a lot.

Then he rotated his hand so his fingers just framed the side of my breast. He wasn't cupping me, but he was letting me know that he wanted to. I arched up, presenting myself.

Do it. Do it, please.

He must have heard my desperate thought, because he moved fractionally until the weight of my breast was in his palm. God, he felt so warm, almost hot, even through my bra and T-shirt. I whimpered.

"You feel so good," he said brokenly against my lips.

"Mmm," I said, arching my back again.

He squeezed me there, squeezed my breast so gently, molding the roundness of it in his hand. His thumb traced across my pulsing nipple. I jerked and gasped.

I thought he'd want to disappear into the bedroom at that point, but instead he continued to tease my nipple by brushing it over and over again until I was whimpering mindlessly with pleasure. His head bent down until he was breathing hard against the crook of my neck as he continued to torment my nipple. I buried my fingers in his curly, soft hair.

"Nova," he whispered roughly. "I want more. Do you want more?"

"Yes." My voice sounded so breathy I hardly recognized it.

"Bedroom." He scooped me into his arms.

"Gage, no! You're going to hurt yourself." Neither of us was completely well from our bout of stomach flu.

Gage snorted. "I'm fine. You hardly weigh a thing."

I knew that wasn't true, but I decided not to argue. He carried me from the kitchen with a hot look of concentration on his face. I'd never seen him look quite like that before. It was incredibly exciting.

In his arms I was very close to his face. Close to his beautiful mouth. He had the most gorgeously shaped lips I'd ever seen. They were like a work of art in themselves. Halfway down the hall, I pulled his head down to mine and kissed him. I couldn't resist it.

"Mmm. Baby, I can't see where I'm going." He bumped into a wall. The crash of a picture hitting the floor.

I didn't care. We continued kissing. Our mouths were desperate now, sucking and biting and licking, and Gage bumped into the wall again. He reached the door of the bedroom and kicked it open and suddenly I was falling onto the mattress.

Chapter 25
So Good

He pounced on me. Growling. I laughed and wriggled beneath him and he pinned my legs with his. He grabbed my arms and pulled them over my head.

"You're lucky I'm not going to punish you for laughing," he said, and once more took my mouth with his.

My core was on fire. I ached for him, and the way he was dominating me at the moment made me even hotter. My hips undulated against him, wordlessly begging him for more.

This was a mistake and I knew it. If we had sex, it would bind me to him, at least in my own mind. In my heart. And we wouldn't stay together. We didn't belong together, not really.

But I was here now, and he was laying over me, and all I wanted was to feel him inside me. No matter how crazy it was, I'd go through with it, just to be with him this one time.

He pulled up my shirt, exposing my bra. It was just an old beige thing, completely utilitarian. It didn't even have a little bow in the center or anything. I flushed and tugged at my hem so I could cover it.

"Don't do that," he said. "I want to look."

"It's just an old piece of junk."

"It's covering you. That makes it beautiful."

God, where did he come up with these lines? Did he steal them from his movies or what?

"Take the shirt off," he said. "please."

My tongue came out to moisten my lips and his nostrils flared. I stripped off the T-shirt. Gage undid the clasp of my bra with a flick of his fingers and it sprang apart, baring my breasts completely.

The blue of his eyes turned to smoky slate. His lips parted as he stared at my naked torso and my hands twitched with the desire to cover myself. He grabbed them.

"Don't you dare," he said. "I want to see you. Every part of you."

"But—"

"You're so fucking beautiful, Nova." His head descended and he took my aching nipple into his mouth.

Wet heat and a powerful tugging sensation brought me part way off the bed with a loud cry. He chuckled against my flesh and continued sucking on me. His hand cupped me, gently molding and squeezing as he suckled. Every pull on my nipple sent an exquisite charge between my breast and my sex, making me ache almost unbearably between my legs.

I was moaning continuously now. And gasping. My fingers clutched his hair; my legs moved restlessly beneath him. If I'd been standing, I probably would have fallen to the floor.

He switched to the other breast, beginning all over again with the brushing. The man had amazing patience. And he was going to drive me crazy, really crazy, before we were done.

I was okay with that.

Leaving my breasts, he kissed his way down my belly, pausing at the waistband of my yoga pants. His fingers curled around the elastic and he looked at me, a question in his eyes.

"Yes," I said.

"Lift your hips."

I complied and he pulled down my pants, tossed them to the floor. We did the same with my panties. God, I was easy. And I didn't care. All I wanted was this time with him, before I had to give him up.

"Beautiful legs, too," he murmured, running his hands up the sinuous lines of my calves.

This time I didn't even try to argue, although I thought he was wrong. My legs weren't beautiful. They were too short, too muscular, too ... too Nova.

He bent his head and pressed his lips to the inside surface of my left calf. I sighed. Smiling against my skin, he continued kissing me, moving upward toward my knee. Over my knee. Up my inner thigh.

Was he going to ...? Yes, he was.

His tongue emerged and gave me a delicate lick along the center of my folds. I yelped. He laughed softly, and I felt the puffs of his breath on my sex. I never would have thought that would be erotic, but it was.

With his thumbs, he parted me. His tongue slid more firmly across my center and I moaned.

"Damn, you taste good," he growled against me.

That was possibly the hottest thing any guy had ever said to me. I moaned again and he pierced me with his tongue. I arched my back.

"Gage!" Now my voice sounded completely unrecognizable. "Gage! Please."

"Please what, baby?" He sounded amused, the jerk.

"Keep—oh, God, please keep doing that." Where Gage was concerned, I had no shame at all.

"That's what I want to hear." He teased me for a moment, exploring each fold and crevice of me before plunging back into my sheath with that talented tongue of his.

A fleeting thought occurred to me—that it was a good thing we were so far apart from any neighbors. Because I was making enough noise to rouse a whole city neighborhood. Out here on the mountain, no-one would hear me yelling my head off as Gage made me come.

A long masculine finger slipped inside me while he continued to lick me. He bent the finger. That was all it took to send a vicious spike of ecstasy through me, to make me shatter in the biggest orgasm I'd ever had.

When I came down, I noticed he was smiling up at me. He looked unbearably smug, and I was so besotted with him I thought it was cute. He looked happy, happier than I'd ever seen him.

"Wow," I said breathlessly. "That was ... I don't even have words."

"Amazing," he said. He moved up until he was lying beside me. "Incredible. Unforgettable."

"All those things."

"For me too." He bent down to kiss me.

He tasted musky, tangy, a strange and foreign flavor that could only be me. I'd never tasted myself before. On him, it was sexy as hell.

"You're overdressed," I whispered as he paused. I grabbed the hem of his shirt. "May I?"

"Anytime, Nova."

I smiled as I sat and pulled the shirt up, over his head. Now that incredible, amazing body of his was bared to me and I wanted to savor the moment. I dropped the shirt over the side of the bed and lifted my hands to his chest.

Beneath his lightly furred skin, he was all hard muscle and bone. I remembered how I'd found him, how I'd stripped him and laid down with him. How cold he'd been. Cold like death.

Now he was warm. I stroked the broad, hard planes of his chest and brushed my palms over his nipples. His breath caught. I leaned in and kissed him just beneath his collarbones.

His eyes were even smokier than they'd been before, his lips parted, slightly glossy from all our kissing. He watched me as I covered him with kisses, as I stroked him over his shoulders, his arms, his ribs, his narrow waist. I tugged at the waistband of his sweats until I got them down a couple of inches and then I kissed him beneath his navel. Right on the line of hair that pointed the way to his cock.

His erection made a tent in his sweatpants.

"Lift up," I said.

"You don't have to, Nova. I don't mind if we stop now."

"That's very sweet and gentlemanly, but I want this," I said. "So unless you don't, you'd better lift up."

He smiled and lifted his hips for me. I pulled down his pants and his fully erect cock sprang out.

He was huge. When I'd seen him before, he'd been icy cold and on the brink of death. Now he was very much alive and highly aroused. It made an enormous difference ... no pun intended.

He was so big I probably could have grasped him in two hands, one over the other, and still had a bit of him to spare. He was thick, too. The slightly spongy head was already pearled with a drop of pre-come.

I bit my lip. Glanced at him. His gaze was still fixed on me, even more intently now. I bent my head and licked him, right across the very tip, taking that drop of pre-come onto my tongue.

Gage groaned. "Nova."

He tasted good. I opened my mouth and took him inside. He stretched me, pushed my jaws apart until they almost hurt. I felt him hit the back of my throat and fought back the gag reflex.

"Jesus, babe, you don't have to do that."

Yeah, whatever. I was so doing this.

I released him from my mouth and gave him a thorough licking, from base to tip and all around the head. Then I took him in my mouth again, tasting him at the back of my throat. He smelled and tasted like sex.

This—he—could be inside me. Maybe he would be, soon. The thought of his giant cock moving inside my pussy instead of only in my mouth made my whole body ache with longing and I moaned. I wanted that, wanted it now.

"You need to stop," he gasped. "Or I'll—"

I released him. I would have let him come in my mouth, but I wasn't sure I'd get another chance to have him inside my pussy. I couldn't pass that up.

"Do you have any condoms?" he said.

Shit. I could have smacked myself in the forehead. Birth control! No, wait ...

"I have a patch." I'd almost forgotten about it since I'd broken up with Barry and sex had become a non-issue. I pointed to the tiny thing stuck to my arm.

"You don't mind if we do without? I'm clean," he said. "I swear. I get checked once a month."

Whoa. That said something about his sex life that I didn't want to examine just now.

"I don't mind," I said. I'd think about that other thing later.

"Come here." He dragged me up to him.

Our mouths clung and devoured as he rolled me under him. I spread my thighs so he could settle between them. Right where I wanted him. Well, almost where I wanted him.

"I want you to be sure," he murmured.

"I'm sure."

He stared down at me, his dark blue gaze suddenly serious. "Really? I won't be mad—"

"Gage, I already told you I want to do this with you. Please? I want you more than I've ever wanted anyone." I reached down between us to take him in my hand.

He trembled. I took his cock and guided it to my entrance.

"I want you to take me," I said.

"Then I will."

With a thrust of his hips, he entered me. I was wet and ready, but his size shocked me. He stretched me to my utmost, and he was so long that his tip almost seemed to bump painfully against my cervix. For an instant, I tensed, afraid.

Then he withdrew, slowly. So slowly. A long, aching glide out and out and out. A pause at my entrance. Then another long slide into my depths.

This time, all I felt was an explosion of delight. I yelled as my head tipped back. He was a perfect fit. I needed all that length and breadth to hit my pleasure points.

"Are you okay?" he rasped.

"Yeah. Oh, yeah! Keep going."

With a crooked grin, he did as I commanded. His hips thrust in a perfect, slow rhythm. His hard cock stroked every nerve ending in my sheath, sending me into spasms of ecstasy so sharp I could do nothing but cry out. Over and over.

"So good, Nova," he said, his gaze fierce. "So tight and hot and wet. Perfect."

His words sent me into another orgasm. I dug my nails into his back as it rocketed through me; I worked my hips against his, begging him for more. By now I was sobbing and groaning incoherently, my voice nothing but animal noises.

"Fuck," he said. "Fuck, baby."

He lost the slow glide. His hips pounded me, his cock pumping into me as he growled above me. I spread my legs as far as they would go, clutching him and crying and pushing up against him.

Gage caught my right leg and lifted it until I wrapped it around his waist. The pose opened me even more, allowed him to penetrate me more deeply until he seemed to reach all the way up to my heart.

When he thrust into me in that position, I lost my mind. It was too much, too good, too everything. My nails scratched viciously at his back as I shrieked my ecstasy, as I fell apart.

My body seemed to dissolve from my sex outward. I simply fell apart. I was nothing, no-one, just a point of blissful awareness impaled by him.

He made a strange, growling shout. His head fell back, the tendons in his neck standing out in sharp relief. His powerful arms trembled, his whole body shuddered over mine. His perfect rhythm fell apart, became uneven and uncontrolled as he poured himself into me.

I held him through it. I wrapped both my legs around his waist and grabbed the hard curves of his ass and held on. He continued to groan and shudder for a full minute.

It was an epic orgasm, at least from my perspective. I'd been with Barry and a couple of other guys, and none of them had come quite like Gage did. He was totally lost, consumed, his eyes rolled back in his head, his mouth pulled taut in a grimace that would have looked ugly on anyone else. On him it looked primal. Hot.

When he finally stopped shaking, he paused, his breath coming in long, hard pants, and stared down at me with soft eyes. I didn't know what to say, so I just stared back. No-one had ever made me feel the way he did. He was going to be an addiction for me; I could tell. More sex than this single encounter would probably ruin me for anyone else. But I couldn't tell him that. It would scare him away.

Chapter 26
Afterglow

He lowered himself to me, keeping his weight off me but pressing his whole hot length against me. His mouth captured mine in a hot, wet kiss, which I returned with enthusiasm. Damn. I'd just had two of the best orgasms of my life, and I was getting turned on all over again.

"I could do that with you all day and all night," he said, kissing my cheek.

"Hmm. Me too." That's it, Nova. Express appreciation and enjoyment, while still remaining cool about it all.

"Did you—I mean, you seemed to enjoy it, but—"

I laughed. "Are you serious? I came twice in one night. That's never happened before."

His unsure expression turned self-satisfied. "I thought you were having a good time."

"The best. Ever."

"Really?" He grinned.

"Absolutely." My hand went up to his face, traced the line of one high cheekbone and down, over his stubble to the sharp line of his jaw, visible even through several days' growth of beard.

"I can shave it off if you want," he said.

"No, I like it."

He withdrew from me and I sighed at the loss. Then he pulled me into his arms as he rolled to his side. "I feel the same way, you know," he said, so softly I almost didn't hear him.

"The same way?" I tilted my head back to watch his face.

"Yeah. About you. About this. It was the best. Ever."

Wow. Now I really didn't know what to say. The evil, insecure part of me still wondered if he were feeding me a line, but the rest of me danced around in joy, thinking that maybe he really could be mine. It was all too confusing, so I pulled him down for another kiss.

"When the storm is over, I'm going to have to get in touch with my people," he said. "It's not fair to keep them wondering what happened to me."

"I know."

His big chest expanded on a sigh. "If I had a choice, I'd stay here with you."

"Would you? Why?" God, what a dumb question. "Don't answer that. I mean, if you don't want to. I wish you could stay, too."

He laughed. "Are you sure?"

"Of course I'm sure."

His arm tightened around my back. "Sometimes I wish I could stop. Just walk away, do something else for a living."

"Why can't you?"

He glanced into my eyes. "Because it's not that simple. Because of that thing I told you about the other day, and no, I don't want to talk about it right now. Because I have no idea what else I'd do. Acting is all I've ever known."

"Do you like it?"

His hand made a long, soothing sweep up and down my back. "Yes and no. I love diving into a character, understanding him, living in his world. I love meeting and working with so many different people. But the stress, the pretensions, feeling like I'm constantly on show. That part is the part I hate."

"Have you been mobbed for autographs?"

"Oh, yeah. Not too long ago at a restaurant. Someone recognized me and in five minutes the whole place turned into a stampede. It wasn't pretty."

"I'm sorry. I can only imagine how hard that must be."

"Some of my movies have been really big in international markets, too, so it's not like I can go to some foreign country and be anonymous. The moon might work, though."

"Hey, you should buy a vacation house there. I'd visit you."

He laughed again. "I could have a secret base on the dark side."

"Awesome. Then you'd truly understand the power of the dark side." I spoke the last part of the sentence in my best Darth Vader voice.

"You're good at that." He grinned. "Maybe you should go into acting too."

"Nah. I'd hate it. Men would be throwing themselves at me all the time. It'd be a total drag."

"They would."

I poked him in the ribs. "I was only kidding."

"Well, I'm not."

"Gage, you should stop giving me all those compliments. It's messing with my head."

"Good. You think too little of yourself. It makes me wonder about that douchebag boyfriend of yours."

"Ex-boyfriend. And I thought he was a douche-canoe, not a douchebag."

"Right. Didn't he ever tell you how gorgeous and sexy you are?"

"Not very often. Okay, no. He didn't."

"Ass."

I laughed. "Yeah. I guess it's actually a good thing I caught him cheating, huh?"

"I'd say it is. Otherwise, you wouldn't have met me."

I grinned up at him, enjoying the teasing sparkle in his eyes. But then I realized he was right. If Barry had been faithful, I wouldn't have been living in this cabin. I wouldn't have been here to pull Gage out of the river. We'd have never met. Someone else might have rescued him, or he might have died in that icy water.

The thought of Gage dead, of him drifting away, succumbing to the cold with no-one to care or help him, made me feel sick.

"I'm glad Barry is a douchebag," I said. "Because now I have—I mean, now I've met you."

That possessive verb had just slipped out and I wished I could take it back. I didn't want him to feel pressured. I'm not sure why I was so nervous about that, except I worried he'd think I was some kind of gold-digger. Trying to trap him into a relationship, maybe even a marriage. I figured there must be a lot of fans who'd do almost anything to have a chance to marry Gage Dalton.

He didn't seem to notice my mistake, though. He just smiled thoughtfully as his fingers combed through my hair. "Maybe we should call him when we get out of here. Let him know what a favor he's done us."

I snorted. "Sure. Go ahead."

"I will if you want me to."

"No, you wouldn't. He'd probably tell everyone he knows. Either that or he'd think it was just a prank and ignore it."

Gage dragged his thumb across my lower lip. "Do you want him to know?"

"I couldn't care less." It was true. I was so over Barry that I could hardly remember what his face looked like.

The moment I'd seen Gage, Barry had almost disappeared for me. It was strange, really, because Gage might have been dead for all I knew at that moment. But that hadn't mattered. I'm not sure what that says about me as a person, but there it is. I fell in love with Gage's nearly-dead self.

Oh, God. Love? Had I just thought the L-word?

No. No, I couldn't let myself go there. I could not fall in love with a Hollywood god who'd probably forget me a week after he got home.

"Because of that problem I told you about, it wouldn't be safe for me to bring you with me," he said. "But I wish I could."

"You do?"

"Yeah. Don't sound so surprised."

"It's just—like I said, I'm plain old Nova and you're you."

"Goddamn it, Nova. Quit calling yourself that," he growled, his thick dark brows descending.

"Sorry. But it's true. I'm a nobody."

"You're not a nobody. You're Nova Pennyman, one of the most important people in my life."

He pinched his eyes shut as his lips compressed to a thin line. The distress on his face was hard for me to see. He'd said I was important to him. But in the next instant, he'd also made it clear in one facial expression that he devoutly wished that wasn't true.

"I don't want to hurt you," he said in a harsh whisper, eyes still closed.

"Gage, you won't hurt me. Why do you think you will? I just don't understand." Mainly because he refused to explain things to me.

"You're not going to fool me into telling you," he said.

"Well, since you choose not to tell me, I'm choosing not to believe you when you say I'm important to you."

He rose up on one elbow, glowering down at me. "It's because you're important to me that I'm not telling you."

"That's kind of like what parents say to their kids. This hurts me more than it hurts you. I'm only doing it for your own good." I shook my head at him. "I'm not buying it. You don't trust me. That's what's really going on here."

"Not true." He sat up in bed and ran his fingers through his hair. "That's just not true, Nova. I trust you more than I've ever trusted anyone."

"But not enough to tell me the truth about whatever this terrible secret is." I sat up too.

"It's not a matter of trust. I'm trying to protect you."

"Yeah, you already said that. But don't you think I'm capable of deciding for myself whether I want to take a risk for you? Don't you know I'd do anything for you?"

I flushed hotly. I'd skirted awfully close to the L-word there, and I had no idea what he'd do if it slipped out of me. Get up and run? Refuse to speak to me? Try to talk me out of it?

He took me by the shoulders and stared intently into my eyes. "You have no idea what you're talking about. You can't know whether you're willing to take a risk if you have no idea what that risk is."

"I would if you explained it to me."

"No. I can't do that." He got out of bed and paced, naked, back and forth across the room. "If you keep pushing me, I'm going to get pissed. Like seriously furious, Nova. You don't want to see me like that."

"Why not? Do you turn into a giant green guy or something?"

He paused and looked at me blankly for a second before snorting a laugh. "You know what I mean."

"I hate seeing you so worried, so alone, so down and hopeless," I said, willing him to believe me. "It hurts."

"God. I knew I shouldn't make love to you," he muttered, pacing again.

"What?" My stomach fell about a mile.

He regretted being with me. I pulled the sheet up to my collarbones as a ridiculous excuse for armor. It was absurd, but it was the only thing I had. If he wished we hadn't made love, then I didn't want him seeing me naked anymore.

"No, baby, that's not what I meant," he said. "Making—having sex— it connected us, made us feel things we might not have felt if we'd just stuck to kissing. I want that connection. But it's not good for you. I shouldn't have let it happen."

"Well, I'm glad it did." I crossed my arms over the sheet and scowled at him.

He sighed and subsided to the bed, opening his arms to me. "Come here."

Like a fool, I went to him. He was going to hurt me, that was obvious. He didn't want to. I didn't want him to. But he'd do it just the same. Whether it would happen because of this awful secret of his, or simply because he kept pushing me away in an attempt to protect me, I didn't know. I only knew the pain was on its way.

Chapter 27
Regret

A week later, the sky was clear. Not a single cloud marred the blue. We'd had breaks in the snow during the eight days Gage had stayed with me, but this was the longest one yet. It had stopped the afternoon before, and now with the blue sky, I was pretty sure the storm—or sequence of storms—was officially over.

Our food stores were getting low, but soon we'd be able to get out of the cabin and buy more. I made us pancakes to celebrate, even though I felt like I had a giant lump of lead where my heart should be. The bright weather meant he would leave me soon.

We'd had eight days together, some of them marred by illness but still a long stretch of intimate talks and music. He'd taught me a bunch of new songs. Then there were the drawings I'd made of him. He knew about two of them, but one I'd done while he was asleep. I'd kept that one to myself. All that friend stuff, punctuated by sex. Lots of sex for the past two days.

It felt like we were more than just friends with bennies. Like maybe we had something deeper, something moving into girlfriend-boyfriend territory. I was addicted to him already. Unfortunately, he still wouldn't come clean about those dangerous associates of his.

"What are you going to do when I'm gone?" he said as I set his plate in front of him.

"You don't waste time, do you?" I set a plate in front of my own chair.

Gage shrugged. "Just wondering. I think you should go home. Or maybe go back to school. Living out here isn't right for you."

"Yeah, well...." I stuck my fork in a pancake and pushed it from one side of my plate to the other.

Gage poured maple syrup over his. "I'll worry about you if you stay here. I'll keep thinking of you all alone in this cabin. You never know what might happen around here. Some strange guy might float down the river or something and end up on your living room couch."

I tried to smile for him. "I think that was a once in a lifetime experience."

"You're probably right. But some other weirdo might show up." He frowned at me as he cut a bite of pancake. "I'm serious. It's not safe for you."

"Now you sound like my mother."

"Your mother must be a wise woman."

I rolled my eyes. "I'll be fine, Gage. You don't need to worry about me. Remember how that connection between us is dangerous for me?" Yeah, I sounded a little bitter.

He stuck the pancake in his mouth. Chewed. Closed his eyes and chewed some more. "Shit, these are good."

"Sourdough."

"You're a talented woman."

"I know. And I'm glad you like them." I seemed to have lost my appetite. But I poured a little syrup on my plate and cut a bite anyway.

Hopefully, the joy of homemade sourdough pancakes had derailed Gage from his argument. I had no intention of staying here, but I wasn't going to tell him that. Because he had no right to tell me what to do. And after all that stuff about our connection endangering me, I wasn't interested in hearing how much he'd worry about me.

**

At noon, we heard an engine nearby. We were in the living room, reading and mostly ignoring each other. Things were awkward now and I was beginning to wonder if Gage wasn't right. We shouldn't have had sex. Made love. Whatever it was we'd done together, it had changed our relationship and now things were strained between us.

At the sound of the vehicle, we both looked up and locked gazes. Gage raised his eyebrows at me. I wasn't sure what that was supposed to mean.

"Do you think it's somebody coming for you?" I said.

"No. How would they know where to look? I have no idea who it is." He got up and peered out the window at the snow-covered yard.

I joined him. That particular window looked out on the side of the cabin farthest away from the road, though, so there wasn't much to see.

"I'm going to look out the kitchen window," I said, and turned to go.

He didn't try to stop me. I'm not sure why I thought he would. I guess it was the sense that our strange, snowy idyll was about to end. My silly heart wished he would take me in his arms and tell me he'd never let me go. But that's not how things work in the real world, is it?

From the kitchen, I could see about thirty yards up the long drive that led to the highway. Someone was at the far end in a truck fitted with a snow plow. They were clearing away the snow so I wouldn't be trapped in my cabin.

I smiled. It was probably Joe from Joe's General Store. He was a really, genuinely nice guy about my dad's age who'd already helped me more than I could ever repay, just in advice alone. He'd probably be spending the next few days digging people out.

Gage came up behind me and rested his hand on my shoulder. "You know that guy?"

"Yeah. It looks like Joe's truck. I should find some money so I can pay him." I turned away from the window.

"Nova."

"Yeah?" I gave Gage a careless glance over my shoulder.

He looked worried and sad. "I don't want things to end between us."

"Well, I guess they have to," I said, although the words nearly stuck in my throat. "It's too dangerous for us to be together, right?"

"Yeah," he said, bending his head. "Right."

"I'm sure we'll both get over it." I patted his hand. "Now I have to find something so I can pay Joe."

"You know once people find out I'm here, the media will find a way to harass you."

"I know. But I can deal with it."

The worried look hadn't left his face. "Can you? Have you ever been at the center of something like that?"

"No, but—"

"They say all kinds of shit. Things that aren't true. Things that are true. They'll run the most unflattering pictures of you they can find. Not that they would be able to find any of you, because you're so fucking gorgeous, but still...."

"It's sweet of you to care," I said. "But I'll be fine. I don't care what pictures they run or what they say." I never paid attention to that kind of crap anyway.

Chapter 28

Snow Plow

Gage:

Peering through the window, I could just make out a truck along Nova's drive. A bend in the drive almost concealed it from view, but a little of its blue paint showed through gaps in the trees and the deep rumble of a diesel engine carried easily into the cabin. It had a huge, red snowplow attached to its front end. The driver moved it back and forth methodically, clearing the snow away and creating a berm along one side.

He was going to be at the cabin soon. And then Nova and I wouldn't be alone anymore. Our protected little bubble would burst and the world would descend on us.

I'd known it would happen, sooner or later. But later was what I'd hoped for, and later was apparently now. Which sucked. It meant I'd have to leave her. Soon.

Jesus. The thought of walking away from her made my chest hurt almost as badly as it had when I'd found Jeremy. I didn't want to do it. If there had been any practical way to stay, I'd stick around, keep hiding out here just to be with her.

But word was about to leak regarding my whereabouts.

This Joe guy might very well blab to everyone he knew about seeing me at Nova's. And they'd tell all their friends, and so forth, until everyone in this part of Oregon knew exactly where I was. We'd probably get all kinds of visitors, "just checking in to see if Nova was okay."

Any excuse I had to avoid contacting my people would be gone, just like that. Because I'd have access to a phone. Dozens of phones, probably. Unless maybe all the lines on the mountain were down. I hoped they were.

I glanced at Nova out of the corner of my eye. She was watching Joe's truck make its way through the thick snow, a closed look on her face. She didn't want me to know what she was thinking. Or feeling.

Did she want the same thing I did? I thought we'd established that last night, but at breakfast she'd seemed so mad at me. I wasn't sure what I'd done wrong. Did she not want me to worry about her?

No, she wanted me to spill my guts to her. Even more than I already had. She wanted me to reveal everything there was to know about The Deal, and I couldn't do that.

What would happen if I told her? She was already in danger just from knowing me, from creating an emotional bond with me.

Yeah, so what difference would it make? Go ahead and tell her.

I reached out and caught her hand. She looked up at me, her face free of expression. Still pissed off, then.

"Nova, I want—"

Her fingers curled around mine. "It's all right. I understand."

She didn't. Not at all.

I stared down at her. This might be one of the last times I'd ever see her, and I wanted to remember. I wanted to engrave every detail on my mind, so I could take them out later and examine them. Treasure them.

Her elfin face looked solemn, her pretty mouth turned down a bit at the corners. She had no make-up, as usual. Huge, honey-gold eyes fringed in dark lashes gazed at me, calmly, pretending nothing was wrong. But I knew better.

I cupped her face in my hand. She was so tiny compared to me; my hand covered nearly the entire side of her head. A yearning came over me, to tell her everything, every single thing that had happened to me since I was ten and my mom made The Deal.

Just the idea of telling made the burden lift from my shoulders a tiny bit, and for an instant I could breathe more fully. To share with someone the awful position I was in. To not be alone anymore.

I opened my mouth to confess it all to her. And then I felt it. A *waiting*, a watching from the corner, a dark gloating presence observing us. The hair on the back of my neck all rose at once and I shivered.

He was here. He was watching us, watching me, waiting for me to make a mistake. Waiting for me to involve an innocent woman, just so he could have the pleasure of destroying her.

"What is it?" Nova raised her hand to cover mine, her brows coming together.

"Nothing." I dropped my hand from her face. "It's nothing. I—never mind."

Was that disappointment I saw in her eyes? Damn, it hurt to see that. If I could just explain myself, maybe she'd forgive me. But in explaining, I'd further endanger her and that could not happen.

Better she be disappointed in me than that *he* take her. I couldn't stand that.

I turned from her and pretended to look out the window again. I pretended I gave a shit what was happening out there, when really a huge, ragged hole was opening up in my chest. All I cared about at the moment was that I'd hurt Nova, and I was going to hurt her again, and I was going away, and I'd lost her.

The truth was, I'd never really had her.

This time we'd shared had been a dream in a way. A time apart, separate from everyday reality. An escape. But escapes never last forever. At some point, you always have to face whatever it was you were running from, and for me that point was now.

Joe and his big, blue truck were in the yard now. He saw us looking out the window and waved. Nova waved back. I just clenched my jaw.

He was older, probably in his mid-forties at least. So not a rival. Probably not, anyway. Maybe Nova liked older men. I'd never thought to ask her.

Shit, what was I thinking? We weren't meant to be together, and it didn't matter whether Joe liked her or not. It didn't matter if she liked him. Because I wasn't going to be a part of her life, so jealousy was just stupid.

Knowing that didn't make me feel any better, or any less jealous.

"I'm going to talk to him," she said. She went toward the back door, where she kept her coat, leaving me at the window.

I could stay in here. Hide. Maybe then he wouldn't realize I was here ... except he'd already seen me through the window. He'd ask Nova about me, and I didn't want to force her to lie for me.

Fuck. It was time to man up.

She came back in boots and a coat. She didn't look at me as she opened the front door and waded into the snow accumulated on the front steps. The silent treatment. Great.

Joe climbed out of the cab of his truck. He was tall and burly, with graying brown hair under a baseball cap. He grinned at us.

"Nova! Sorry I couldn't get here earlier, but with the storm—"

"Don't apologize," she said. "I didn't expect you to come at all."

He frowned at her. "We'd never leave you out here by yourself, all snowed in. You got enough wood? Propane? Kerosene?"

"Yeah, I'm good." She reached into her pocket and withdrew a bill. "This is for plowing the drive."

Now he glared. "Put that away. I'm not taking money from you."

"But that was a lot of work."

"Consider it a favor for a friend." He looked over her head at me. "Do I know you, sir?"

"I don't think so," I said. I stepped forward and held out my hand. "Gage Dalton."

He took my hand with a puzzled look in his brown eyes. Then those eyes widened and a huge grin lit up his face. "Gage Dalton the actor? Holy shit, no wonder you looked familiar. My daughter has the biggest crush on you." He pumped my hand ferociously. "It's good to meet you. Great, actually."

"Same."

"Wow," Joe said. "Too bad Misty's not here. She'd be out of her mind. In fact, she will be out of her mind when she finds out I met you. I asked her if she wanted to come with me this morning, but you know teen-age girls. Dad's not cool enough, or sick enough, or whatever it is these days."

"Tell her I said hi."

"We heard they were looking for you in the area, but like I told my wife, I figured they had it wrong. I mean, what would a big name movie star be doing here? It's not even ski season yet. Well, it wasn't. They'll be mobbing us as soon as the roads are cleared, now that we've got all this powder." He turned red and doffed his cap to run his hands through his cropped hair. "Sorry. I'm rambling."

"No problem. I had some car trouble just when the storm was starting and Nova here helped me out. She let me stay with her."

Joe turned his gaze on Nova. "That must have been exciting for you."

She gave him a forced-looking smile. "I didn't even know who he was. I just knew he needed help."

"Jeez, Nova, you shouldn't take in strangers like that. You could get hurt bad." He glanced at me. "No offense, Dalton. It's just—"

"No offense taken. I told her the same thing. I'm grateful, though, that she was willing to take me in. I'd be frozen solid by now if she hadn't." I'd be dead.

"In fact, Joe, Gage needs a ride to somewhere with a working phone," Nova said. "He's got to call his people and let them know where he is. That he's still alive."

Unreasonable of me to feel like she was pushing me out the door, but that was how I felt.

"Oh, sure." Joe gave both of us an amiable grin. "Sure. You wanna ride with me? I was gonna do a few more drives, but I can drop you off at the store. Our cell signal is pretty strong at the store, so you should be able to get through."

"Sure, that would be great. Thanks, man." I smiled at Nova, still pretending everything was all right. "You should come. You've been cooped up in the cabin even longer than I have."

She pursed her lips, looking unhappy. "That's not necessary. I'm fine here."

"No, you should come," Joe said. "I've got room in the cab for three if we squeeze in tight. Misty and her mom would love to see you."

"Oh. Okay, then." She smiled at him, another fake one. It was weird how well I could read her after just a few days with her. They'd been intense days, though.

"You got a coat, Dalton?" Joe said.

"No. It's a little torn up. I'll just go as I am."

"Okay, then. Hop in. The store's just a ten minute drive away."

We climbed into the truck. It had a bench seat in the front. Nova sat between us because she had the shortest legs. She still wasn't looking at me. Jesus. I never should have told her anything at all. Then we wouldn't be suffering this silence between us.

I wanted her to smile at me. I wanted another kiss before I left, and I had the feeling I wasn't going to get one. It was my fault, but still … was this how it was going to be during our last hours together? We were going to be all stiff and unfriendly, acting like what we'd had together meant nothing?

It damn well meant something to me. What I hadn't quite figured out, but I knew Nova was going to ripple out through my life somehow and change everything. Even if I never saw her after today.

The truck jolted and rocked its way up the drive to the highway. All around us, fir and spruce trees bent their branches toward the ground, weighted by the huge puffs of snow they'd accumulated. Every so often, one of the puffs slipped off and the branch bounced upward, a spray of flakes sparkling in the sunlight.

I was going to miss this place. I'd never been one for camping, or the country, except in the tiniest doses. I'd never imagined myself loving a place like this, and now I did. Because of Nova.

Five minutes later, we turned onto the highway. Joe drove slowly and steadily through the snow. Someone—maybe him—had already plowed a narrow lane for driving, so at least we didn't have to plow our way back to the store. I wondered how long it had taken him to clear the way to Nova's place.

"Um, Joe?" she said.

"Yeah, honey?"

"You can't tell anyone except your family about Gage. And they can't tell anyone at all. He needs his privacy and we don't want to be mobbed by the media. Okay? Can you keep it a secret?"

"Of course I can." He glanced across her to me. "Trying to stay out of the public eye?"

"I'm just trying to protect Nova," I said. "I don't want reporters here harassing her. If they know I spent the storm at her place, they'll be all over her. They can be mean. Really nasty." I fixed him with a stern look. "That's why it's so important you and your family keep the secret. I don't want Nova getting hurt."

"No. I totally agree." He nodded solemnly. "You have my word nobody will hear it from me."

"Thank you."

I wasn't convinced he wouldn't talk. Or his daughter. Teen-age girls aren't exactly known for their discretion. But maybe if I impressed them with the need for secrecy, it would buy us a day or so. Of course, at the rate things were moving, I'd probably be long gone by then.

Nova would have the peace and quiet she craved and I'd be back in L.A..

Chapter 29
General Store

Joe's General Store was a big, barn-like building with graying wood siding and a metal roof. It had a long, covered porch just like so many stores you saw in old pictures and in movies, and a painted wooden sign with the name in red and white. There were a couple of other vehicles in the parking lot, but they were covered with snow and had obviously been there a while.

Joe pulled up at the front door, the engine still running. "You kids go in. I'm gonna finish my plowing."

"Thanks, Joe." I opened my door and got out. The sun glittered on the brilliantly white snow, making it hard to see.

"Remember to keep the secret," Nova said, as she followed me.

"Will do."

Nova shut the truck door. She glanced up at me. The snow where we were standing had been shoveled away and the remainder was packed down, but it was still cold as hell.

"Let's go inside," I said.

"Your nose is turning pink." She grinned and ran for the door.

Inside, it was warm and smelled like something spicy. Gingerbread, maybe. Half the store looked like a small grocery, with ordinary rows of metal shelves covered in cans and boxes, a tiny produce department along one side. The other half had a weird assortment of stuff—clothes, car parts, garden tools, hardware, cosmetics. Probably a bunch of other stuff I couldn't see. I guess they'd really meant it when they'd called it a general store.

A skinny girl with long brown hair hanging down her back stood in the middle of the clothes, folding some sweaters. "I don't see why we have to work today, Mom," she said in a whiny tone, talking to someone I couldn't see. "Nobody's going to come in."

The door slammed behind us and she looked up. For an instant, she seemed annoyed to be proven wrong. Then she looked at me and her face went blank. Another instant, and her eyes went completely round as her mouth fell open.

"Hi, Misty," Nova said. "We need to use your parents' cell phone."

"That's—" Misty pointed at me. "Is he—are you Gage Dalton?"

"Yes. I am, and I really need to use your phone."

"Oh, my God!" She squealed in an ear-drum destroying shriek and jumped up and down, her hair flying. "Oh, my God! Oh, my God! I can't believe this! This can't be happening to me!"

Nova gave me an amused smile. "She knows who you are."

"I can see that."

"Oh, my God! I have to tell Cherie. She won't even believe it!"

Nova shook her head as she walked up to the squealing teen. She took Misty by the forearm. "You can't tell anyone."

Misty frowned at her. "Why not?"

"Because Gage doesn't want anyone to know he's here. He doesn't want reporters coming in and harassing everyone in town."

Misty's shoulders sagged. "Oh. But why not?"

"They'd make a lot of problems for you," I said, giving her one of my charm-the-fans smiles. "They'd be all over your parents' store, interfering with their business. They'd harass Nova. They can be unbelievably nasty sometimes, getting into people's private property and just causing all kinds of trouble. I'm sure you don't want your family to suffer."

"Oh. I never thought of it that way." She gazed at me with wide, star-struck eyes. "I can't tell anyone?"

"Not until I'm long gone."

"Pooh. That sucks."

"Misty?" said an adult woman's voice. "What's going on out here? Are you okay?"

"Yeah, Mom, I'm fine. We have customers."

"I heard you yelling." A plump woman about Joe's age entered the store from a back room. She had brown hair nearly the same shade as Misty's, and she wore jeans and a thick fleece pullover.

She saw us and smiled politely, first at me, then at Nova. "Hello, Nova. It's good to see you. Who's your friend?"

Then she got a closer look at me and her jaw dropped just like Misty's had. "Oh. You're that Gage Dalton guy, aren't you? They've been looking all over for you."

"Yeah," I said. "Your husband drove me and Nova over here so I could use your cell phone. Just so they don't think I died or anything."

"Oh! Of course you can. Anytime. It's right over here."

Apparently, Joe and Marcia used some kind of cell signal boosting equipment to make their cell signal powerful enough out here in the boonies. Soon enough, I had my mother's number dialed. Behind me, Nova patiently explained all over again why Marcia and Misty couldn't tell anyone they'd seen me.

"Hello?" my mom said blearily on the other end of the connection.

"Hi, Mom. It's Gage."

"Gage? Is that really you?" She sounded drunk.

I sighed. Just business as usual for Nancy Dalton. "Yeah, Mom, it's me. I'm alive and well, just snowed in."

"Oh, God. Oh, my God. You're still alive." She started to cry. "I thought you were gone. I thought *he'd* gotten you. Just like he did Jeremy."

"No, he didn't. I'm fine, just like I said." I kept my gaze fastened on the wall of the store, instead of looking at the women.

"Where are you?"

"In Subalpine. It's a little town in the Cascades."

"Wh-when are you coming home?"

"I don't know. The roads are blocked. I don't know how long it'll be."

"Call Cindy. She'll get a helicopter up there for you."

Shit. Cindy was my personal assistant, and she'd probably get a helicopter if I asked her to. She might do it even if I didn't. This had to be stopped.

"Mom, that would just draw attention to me. I don't want that."

"But we need you here."

"I don't want Subalpine taken over by reporters and fans and bullshit. It's not prepared for that."

"Your fans are the reason you're such a big star," she slurred. "You should be grateful to them. You should love each and every one of them."

Great. She was launching onto that lecture again. "Mom," I interrupted. "Mom! I do love my fans. Every one of them. But I don't want people coming up here and intruding on the locals."

She snorted. "If it's like the mountain towns I've seen, they could use the business."

"Just don't call Cindy. I'll do it. I'll make arrangements; don't worry; it might be a few days, though, before I can make it home."

"No. No, we need you here now."

"You'll have to make do without me." I couldn't see what was so pressing that I had to go home immediately. It's not like I had a filming schedule or anything. I was between projects. "It'll be fine. I'll be home as soon as I can."

After I finished with my mom, I called Cindy and explained what was going on. She said she'd send a driver in an SUV to get me as soon as the roads were passable, and that was fine by me. It ought to give me a couple more days with Nova to work things out.

Chapter 30
Always

Nova:

The helicopter showed up at three o'clock in the afternoon. Gage and I were still at Joe's store, where we'd stayed to chat with Misty and Marcia and eat a lunch of sandwiches and hot soup at the tiny table that comprised the store's "cafe." The heavy thucka-thucka-thucka of the chopper's blades came to us from far away, clear in the winter air. Gage's head came up.

He scowled ferociously at the front windows of the store. "They didn't."

"Gage?"

"I told them not to send a goddamn helicopter. And they did it anyway."

"Why didn't you want a helicopter?" I said, exchanging bewildered glances with the other women.

"Because it's fucking disruptive, that's why. 'Scuse my language, Marcia. It makes a ton of noise and gets all kinds of attention I don't want. You don't want." He shoved his fingers through his curly hair. "Fuck. My mom must have called Cindy after I talked to her."

"It'll be fine," Marcia said. "We don't mind. Do we, girls?"

"No!" Misty said in her perky, I'm-talking-to-a-star voice. "Not at all."

I minded. A helicopter would take him away from me even faster than a car. The roaring of its blades got louder every second, and it now sounded as if they were almost on top of us. My heart hurt.

I know it was childish, but I was angry. At him. Angry because he was leaving, because he wasn't taking me with him, because he wouldn't tell me what was bothering him. Because he didn't trust me or believe in me, or maybe because he wanted to get rid of me. I'm sure I could come up with at least a dozen more reasons why I was furious with him.

I sneaked a glance at him. He was shaking his head, still glowering, and drumming his fingers on the table that formed the General Store's "cafe." The latte Marcia had made for him sat almost untasted in front of him.

He was probably used to much better ones down in Cali. Our little town wasn't good enough for him. I gritted my teeth as my blood pressure and heart rate both rose.

Who did he think he was? I'd rescued him. He'd be dead if it wasn't for me. He wasn't too good for me, or Subalpine either. He needed to get over himself.

The roar of the chopper became an ear-torturing scream and the whole parking lot became nothing but whirling snow. At the center of the whirlwind, the chopper gently descended to the pavement. It was a big one, bright white with a blue stripe along its side. Not that I knew anything about choppers—it just looked a lot bigger than ones I used to see flying over Portland.

"Are you sure it's safe for you to fly in this weather?" I said softly.

"There isn't a single cloud in the sky," Gage said. "I'm sure it's safe. Doesn't mean I want to do it, though."

"Do you have to do what they say?" Misty said, wide-eyed.

"He grimaced. "I do have to leave. I've got a lot of work I have to get back to. I just didn't want to do it this way. But now the damage is done and I might as well take advantage of the opportunity to get back to L.A. by tonight."

I bent my head. My heart rate had gone from speeding in anger to almost stopping cold. This chopper thing was an opportunity to him. Maybe I'd been an opportunity too.

The blades of the chopper slowed gradually until they were barely moving and the snow had mostly settled. A middle-aged woman dressed in skinny jeans tucked into knee-high caramel leather boots and a chic white ski jacket climbed out of the cabin and ran through the remaining wind to the store, the pom-pom on her white hat bobbing with her motion. Through the brief opening and closing of the door, I caught a flash of a remarkably luxurious interior.

Gage tugged on the collar of the flannel shirt Marcia had given him and stood. She'd also given him a pair of new jeans and some boots, and he looked like a regular lumberjack. An extremely hot lumberjack.

The door banged open and the middle-aged woman came inside. She stared around the store for a moment, looking lost until her gaze settled on Gage.

"Gage!" she called. "Thank God."

He lifted his hand. "Cindy."

So not his mom, then.

Cindy walked toward him, her boots clacking on the linoleum floor. She had perfectly applied make-up and glossy lips, carefully highlighted blond hair sticking out from under her hat. In fact, she really didn't look middle-aged and I'm not sure what it was about her that had given me that initial impression.

"Nova, this is my personal assistant, Cindy," Gage said. "Cindy, this is Nova Pennyman. I've been staying at her place."

Cindy gave me a dismissive glance, a once-over that took in my disheveled hair, my old jeans and battered coat. Then she turned a brilliant smile on Gage. "You're okay! You look great." She leaned in to press air kisses against each of his cheeks.

"Yeah. Did you know I fell in the McKenzie River? I would have died of hypothermia or drowned if Nova hadn't pulled me out. She saved my life."

I flushed as I felt everyone's gazes turn to me. We hadn't told Misty and Marcia about that, either, so they were as surprised as Cindy.

"Really," she said. "I had no idea."

"I know," Gage said with a chiding smile. "That's why I told you. By the time she got me warm enough, the storm was in full force and the phone lines were down. That's why I wasn't able to call anyone until this morning."

Cindy directed a slightly-less glacial look on me. "You pulled him out of a river?" she said, sounding skeptical.

"Yes, I did."

She glanced at Gage and then back at me. "So how much do you want?"

I gaped at her. "I beg your pardon?"

"How much do you want? I assume you did it for the reward."

"What the fuck?" The obscenity just slipped out of me, but now it was out and I wasn't taking it back. It seemed appropriate. "You don't think anyone would help Gage unless it was for money?"

Cindy flushed beneath her expensive make-up. "Well, I didn't say that. And I didn't mean it that way."

"Nova," Gage said, catching my hand. "It's okay."

"No, it's not. This woman just insulted you."

"I did not insult Mr. Dalton," Cindy said stiffly, lifting her chin. "I merely thought, since we get so many gold-diggers—not that I thought of you that way, but still—there are so many people taking advantage of Mr. Dalton that I naturally assumed—"

Like you're taking advantage of him?

I glared at her. "Listen, Cindy, I had no idea who Gage was when I pulled him out. He was just a guy who needed help. I don't want any money, yours or his."

She took a step backward, holding up her hands in surrender. "Okay. No hard feelings, right? I didn't mean to offend."

"You should be apologizing to Gage, not me."

"Nova—" he said in a warning tone.

She compressed her lips. "You're right. Gage, I'm sorry. I didn't mean that the way it came out."

"I know you didn't," he said. "It's fine. Really. Nova, you need to chill out. I understood exactly why Cindy said what she did."

I dragged my hand away from his. "Fine. I'm chill. I just think you deserve more respect."

"Cindy, will you give us a minute?" he said.

"Oh, sure. Yeah. Take all the time you want."

Gage took me by the elbow. Marcia got up from her chair and introduced herself and Misty to Cindy while he chivvied me across the store and into the clothing aisles.

"Look, Nova, I know you're mad at me," he said, "but don't take it out on Cindy. It's not her fault."

"That wasn't about my being mad at you. I don't think she should talk about you that way."

He gave me a half-quizzical, half-sad smile. "All right. We'll just have to agree to disagree on that."

"Fine." He'd be gone soon, anyway, and my attitude toward Cindy wouldn't matter. Nothing about him would matter anymore. Not to me.

I should probably say at this point that I'm a crappy liar, even when lying to myself. He would always matter to me, no matter where he went. No matter what he did. Even if I never saw or heard of him again, he would matter to me.

But I couldn't tell him that because he didn't want to hear it. He didn't want that kind of bond between us, so I had to keep it to myself.

"So you do admit to being mad at me?" he said, his smile broadening.

I half-shrugged. "Yeah. I guess. I mean, you won't confide in me and I feel like you don't trust me."

His frown reappeared. He looked so damn serious when he did that, like the fate of the world lay in his hands. "I do trust you. Implicitly. This isn't about trust; it's about protecting you. I thought I made that clear."

"Yeah, you did." I patted his arm, a bit awkwardly. How had things gone from the transcendent passion of the last couple days to this chilly distance? "It's okay, Gage. It's not important, anyway, since you're going home."

He gave me another searching look. "If you say so."

"I want you to have a good flight back. I want you to be happy," I said, my throat thick and tight.

"Give me your number," he said. "I'll call you when I get in."

He wanted my number. That was a good sign, right? I dug around in my purse for a pen and scrap of paper, scribbled my number, handed the paper to him.

Gage tucked the paper in the breast pocket of his flannel shirt. "Thank you. I'm sorry I have to leave like this. Really, I am, Nova. I wish I could stay here with you, but I have too many people relying on me. I have to get back."

"Okay. I understand."

"Will you come out to the chopper with me to say good-bye?" He grabbed my hand again, tightly enough so I'd have a tough time getting out of his grasp unless he decided to let me go.

I swallowed. "Okay. Yeah, I can do that."

God, this was happening too fast. Way too fast. I didn't want him to go at all. And from the sorrow in his blue eyes, he didn't want to either. My stomach suddenly rebelled, nausea churning and trying to force my stomach contents up into my esophagus. I took a deep breath through my nose, forcing the nausea back down.

This was all so confusing.

A clack-clack on the echoing floor announced Cindy's approach. She stopped a couple yards away. "Is everything good?"

"Yeah." Gage sounded husky. "We're good."

"Ready to go? Where's your stuff?"

Had she missed the part where I fished him out of the river?

"I don't have any stuff," Gage said. "It's in the rental car, somewhere up the road."

"Do you need it?"

"No, I'm good. You can send someone to get it when the road is cleared."

"So are we ready to get on board, then?" She flicked another chilly glance at me.

No. No, we're not ready.

"Yeah." Gage didn't let go of my hand as he led me toward the door.

Cindy craned her neck around his big frame to frown at me. "Is she coming too?"

"No," Gage said. "We're just saying good-bye."

Cindy's eyes clouded, as if with puzzlement. She couldn't seem to decide what to make of me. I almost laughed. I was probably so far out of her realm of experience I might as well have come from another planet.

Then we were outside and the wind from the chopper blades was blowing our hair in a hundred different directions. Cindy ran right for the aircraft. Gage and I trudged toward it, our hands still clasped tightly. I glanced over my shoulder to see Misty and Marcia on the porch of the store, watching.

Just before we ducked under the blades, Gage spun me toward him and grabbed me in an all-consuming hug. His arms clasped me to him, nearly lifting me off my feet. His head bent down to mine and he nuzzled my ear and kissed me on the cheek.

"I'll never forget you, Nova Pennyman," he said. "Never. You'll always be with me."

"Same here." My eyes stung. I blinked rapidly.

"Hey," he murmured against my ear. "It's going to be all right."

"Sure." My voice sounded choked. I reached into the breast pocket of my parka and pulled out one of the drawings I'd made of him. I wasn't sure why I'd brought it along until now. "Here. I want you to have this."

He studied the paper, looking both sad and pleased. His gaze snapped to mine. "Are you sure you want me to have this?"

"I'm sure."

Gage bent to kiss me again, this time on the lips. "Thank you, baby. I'll frame it when I get home."

Now my eyes really were stinging. Tears pooled, getting ready to run down my cheeks and embarrass the hell out of me. "I love you, Gage."

Oh, shit. The L-word. Much more embarrassing than tears, especially since the confession was unwanted.

Gage froze. For a long moment, he simply held me against his warm, hard body. Then he pressed a kiss to my forehead.

"Be safe," he said.

He released me and ducked under the blades, running hunched over to the craft, my drawing clutched in his hand. The door opened from inside. I watched him climb in and shut the door against me.

He hadn't said it back.

Chapter 31

Helicopter

Gage:

Inside the chopper, I slid into one of the beige leather bucket seats and got buckled in. With the door shut, the cabin was remarkably quiet, the din of the blades muffled by all the sound-proofing and insulation. This was definitely a luxury chopper. It looked more like an airplane inside than the typical helicopter.

I tucked Nova's drawing into my shirt, where it would be safe. Then I turned my head to look out the window. Nova was still there, just standing and watching, long dark hair flying in the icy wind of the chopper blades. She looked so alone, even though Misty and Marcia were just behind her on the porch.

I love you, Gage.

Did I love her back? I couldn't figure out what it was I felt. Anger, joy, terror, grief. All of that, and maybe more. She loved me. No-one had ever said that to me before. But I wasn't worthy of her love, and loving me would endanger her.

Even worse, if I allowed myself to love her in return, *he* would consider her a target.

The feelings Nova inspired in me were everything I'd said I'd never do or feel, and didn't want. For years, I'd lived by the notion that I was immune to love. I'd been so wrong that I wanted to go back in time and smack myself in the head.

It had been easier to tell myself I didn't want love, wasn't interested in a committed relationship, than to admit the truth. That I did want it, yearned for it, and could never have it.

Pressure from beneath me let me know we were lifting off. The ground began to fall away. Nova turned her back on me and walked up the steps to the General Store.

It killed me to see her do that. I shouldn't feel this way about her. We hadn't known each other long enough. For all I knew, she had all kinds of obnoxious qualities that would make themselves known on a longer acquaintance.

I didn't believe that, though. I'd found the girl for me and I had to leave her.

"She's kind of different." Cindy's voice had a hint of snark I didn't like.

"Yeah," I said, still looking out the window at Nova's retreating back. "She is."

"She's not like your usual girls."

I looked over my shoulder at her. "My usual girls don't know how to survive in a snowstorm." My usual girls didn't know how to have a meaningful conversation, either.

Cindy regarded me with a speculative light in her eyes. "You want to talk about it?"

"No." I settled against the seat back.

"It looked like you two had gotten pretty close."

I shot her a sideways glare. "We're friends. That's all."

She muttered something that sounded like "yeah, right." I ignored that in favor of closing my eyes and trying to blank my mind. Just go somewhere with no pain, no sorrow, no guilt.

It didn't work very well. I wanted to tell the pilot to turn the chopper around. I wanted to drag Nova to L.A. with me, whether she wanted to go or not.

I love you, Gage.

If she loved me, she'd want to come with me. Right? But even if that were true, it would put her in a terrible position. I wasn't going to do that to her. I cared too deeply for her.

Did I love her? I wasn't sure what love was supposed to feel like. I'd never told a woman I loved her, except for my mom of course. And that hadn't even happened for years. I'd certainly never said it to a lover.

I'd never given myself a chance to get close enough to a woman to imagine myself in love. So I had no basis for comparison. I was flying blind here.

She was so angry with me for not telling her everything. Should I have confided in her? Was that the loving thing to do? I really wasn't sure. I just wanted to protect her, keep *him* from developing an interest in her.

Cindy and I settled into a prickly silence as the chopper swooped over mountainsides covered in evergreen trees so dark they almost looked black. Less than an hour later, we'd landed in Eugene and boarded the private jet awaiting us. We had almost all the comforts of home, except for Nova.

I blinked and rubbed my forehead at that thought. Was Nova home for me now?

"Would you like a drink?" Cindy said, making right for the bar. She grabbed a bottle of Scotch and held it up for me.

"No, thank you." I'd promised Nova I would quit and I meant it. Maybe we couldn't be together, but that didn't mean I would break my word.

"Really? You sure? You always like a drink when you fly," she said, pouring one for herself.

"I'm sure."

"I'll bet you're glad to get out of that redneck pit," Cindy said as she sat down.

"It wasn't a pit," I said.

"Looked like one to me. I don't think that store had been updated since the sixties."

"They have an espresso machine," I said dryly. "It's been updated."

She laughed. "That's a good one."

"I thought Marcia made a good latte. Not that I normally drink that girly shit."

"I'm surprised she even knew what a latte is," she said in a catty tone. "And that Nova. I'm glad you're just friends, Gage. She wouldn't make a good partner for you."

I raised my eyebrows, struggling to control a surge of irritation. "Who's talking about a partner?"

"You just seemed awfully close to her." She pursed her lips as she applied a fresh layer of gloss.

Was she going to harp on this all the way back to Cali? "You get close when someone saves your life. That's all it is."

Liar.

None of this was any of Cindy's business. She was my assistant, not my mom or my sister and not my girlfriend. I couldn't even figure out why she cared, and I wasn't going to discuss it with her.

I shifted my position and the drawing in my shirt crackled. My life before Nova had been nothing but business and empty partying. There had been no home, no real family. Mom didn't count, as far as I was concerned. She was the one who'd made The Deal and she'd long since lost any sense of home for me. I'd been alone.

Then I'd fallen in that river. Nova hadn't just pulled me out of some cold water and warmed me up, she'd pulled me out of a long, downward spiral of stupid behavior. She'd made me see there were better people in the world than the ones I normally called friends, and I wanted more of that.

I wanted more of her.

Before I could invite her back into my life, though, I had to be worthy of her. I had to make my life a safe place for her. I had to conquer the dark shit that had hung over me for so long I couldn't remember what it was like to function without it.

When I'd found my way out of The Deal, then I could maybe have Nova back. If she'd take me.

The End

Read the exciting second and third books in the Gage and Nova Trilogy!

Bedeviled

Gage: When I walked away from Nova to return to L.A., I thought I was doing the right thing, protecting her from the darkness of my life. But now, I know I can't make it without her. My soul is in hock to the devil, though, and I'd do anything to keep from endangering her. So my mission is clear: find a way out of The Deal. I only hope I can fix the mess before Nova gives up on me.

Nova: I tell myself I'm over Gage, that I don't need him. But I know the truth. I'll never be over him. I'll always love him. He's in L.A. I haven't seen or spoken to him in almost two months. But lately, paranormal events seem to have invaded my life. Something dark and terrifying is stalking me, and it knows his name.

Let yourself get swept away in Gage and Nova's passionate story as they struggle to overcome the barriers that separate them and prevent them from declaring their love.

Breaking Free

Gage: I never should have told Nova I love her.

When I was ten, my mother sold my soul to the devil in return for my success in Hollywood. Turns out you can't sell someone else's soul. But Lucifer took my girlfriend anyway, as compensation for a deal he never honored in the first place. Now the woman I love is in hell because of me, and I'll do whatever I must to rescue her. Even if I have to go to hell myself to bring her back.

Nova: There's something strange about my new neighborhood. The houses, the apartments, the streets seem so empty. Where are all the people? My only companion, Declan, seems as lost as I feel. And while I like Declan, in my dreams I love a man named Gage. If only he were real...

Re-unite with Gage and Nova as they overcome their final obstacles in the haunting final book of the trilogy.

Tori Minard has published fourteen romance and erotic romance novels and three novellas, in addition to a handful of short stories, both under her own name and as Tessa Tremaine. Her series include The Amaki, Legends Of A Dark Empire, Avery's Crossing, Fortunata: The Jhidris Conspiracy, and Tales Of The Demon Kin.

Tori wrote her first story in elementary school, with a lamentable lack of punctuation. In high school, she spent more time writing fiction than doing homework. Her early stories featured demonic dogs, dolls possessed by evil spirits—no, she'd never heard of Chucky—and politically incorrect post-apocalyptic romance.

She discovered science fiction in the sixth grade, with her dad's recommendation of Edgar Rice Burroughs' *At the Earth's Core,* the first book in his Pellucidar series. Prior to that, her reading had included ghost stories, animal stories and adventure tales. Around the same time, she was discovering the joys of erotica by sneaking her mom's books and reading all the naughty bits. Her mom claims to have skipped those parts.

After a long detour for such grown-up pursuits as working boring full-time jobs (State of Alaska, U.S. Postal Service), getting married and having a child, she returned to her first love—storytelling. She was born and raised in Alaska, and now lives in the Pacific Northwest with her husband, son, and micro-dog

Discover other titles by Tori Minard

Tales Of The Demon Kin:
Novellas:
Malefica
Fury Enchained
The Devil You Know
Taken By Storm

Novels:
Lucifer's Castle
Mastered By Love
Taken By Desire

Short Stories:

Stainless Steel Vampire, story number one in the Skye Donovan series
Love Potion Number Ninety, Skye Donovan story number two
If I Should Die; a Legends Of The Dark Empire story
Price of a Rose, a sexy fairy tale (novelette)
Lemon Drop, a sweet erotic toy possessed by a sex spirit

Amaki Novels:

The Heart Moon
Dragon Moon
Blood Moon

Avery's Crossing Novels:

Rush
Bad Company (Gage and Nova Book 1)
Bedeviled (Gage and Nova Book 2)
Breaking Free (Gage and Nova Book 3)

Fortunata Novels:

Dirty Magic

Legends Of A Dark Empire Novels:

Temple Of The Heart
Darkness Awakened
Darkness Forbidden
Darkness Beloved
Darkness Embraced

Connect with Tori online

To learn more about Tori, visit her blog at http://www.toriminard.com
Twitter: http://twitter.com/#!/ToriMinard
Facebook: http://www.facebook.com/toriminard.paranormalromance
Pinterest: http://www.pinterest.com/toriminard/